DRAW THE CURTAIN CLOSE

THE "MAC" SERIES

Draw the Curtain Close (1947)
Every Bet's a Sure Thing (1953)
The Case of the Murdered Model (1954, aka *Prey for Me*)
The Mean Streets (1954)
The Brave, Bad Girls (1956)
You've Got Him Cold (1958)
The Case of the Chased and the Chaste (1959)
How Hard to Kill (1962)
A Sad Song Singing (1963)
Don't Cry for Long (1964)
Portrait of a Dead Heiress (1965)
Deadline (1966)
Death and Taxes (1967)
The King Killers (1968, aka *Death Turns Right*)
The Love-Death Thing (1969)
The Taurus Trip (1970)

THE PETE SCHOEFIELD SERIES:

And When She Stops (1957 aka *I.O.U. Murder*)
Go To Sleep, Jeannie (1959)
Too Hot For Hawaii (1960)
The Golden Hooligan (1961, aka *Mexican Slayride*)
Go, Honeylou (1962)
The Girl with the Sweet Plump Knees (1963)
The Girl in the Punchbowl (1964)
Only on Tuesdays (1964)
Nude in Nevada (1965)

DRAW THE CURTAIN CLOSE

THOMAS B. DEWEY

WILDSIDE PRESS

CHAPTER 1

There was a mile and a half of private drive from the street up to the house. I took it in low gear, trying to figure out why I was coming at all. He was not my type of client. He was not anybody I wanted to have anything to do with.

On the other hand, there was that old score between us that I doubted he would remember. What I was afraid of was that I would remember and make an unsmart move.

I stopped thinking about it. It only gave me indigestion and a warm collar. I shifted into second, rounded the last curve and pulled up under the portico. I climbed out of the car, walked up the steps and found a bell to ring.

The guy who opened the door was seven feet tall. He wore a butler's livery but his face didn't follow through. It was the face of a pug and I remembered it without placing the name.

He nodded once at my card and stood aside. I stepped into a reception hall roughly the size of the Trianon. A wide circular staircase went up out of the middle of it and disappeared somewhere. There were high-backed, carved oak chairs against the white walls and a mirror big enough for a man on horseback to get a full view of himself and his mount. At the same time. Opposite the door I had come in was another door and this butler made his way to it hugely. I followed.

The door led into the library. It was a real library, with books, thousands of them, all around a room which resembled the main concourse of the Chicago Public. It was dark-paneled and the ceiling, supported by foot-thick beams, looked very far away.

The butler went out, leaving me just inside the closed door. I looked across all that space to where Warfield sat behind a mahogany desk built in proportion to the rest of the house. I couldn't see him clearly. The lamp threw a white glow over the top of the desk and left his face in shadow.

"Is there a transit system?" I asked, "or do I take a cab?"

I heard his voice then for the first time in my life—a low voice that crackled, like a man eating peanut brittle.

"It's not as far as it looks," he said, "—coming in. It might seem kind of far going out."

He didn't have to spell it for me. I thought back over that long and lively career and wondered how many had found it too far going out.

I made the trek toward the desk, taking my time to show him I wasn't rattled. And I wasn't. But I wasn't easy in my mind either. There was no good reason for a man like Warfield to send for an operative like me. I hadn't liked it from the start and I didn't like it now, but I had to take that one long chance, just in case. I have to live.

There was a leather chair near the desk. From beside it I could look through the big window behind him. The place was on a bluff, far out on the North Shore. It was dark now, but through the window I could see the murky grayness that hung in a thick, motionless cloud out over the lake.

He stood up when I got to the chair. He didn't offer to shake hands. I had the feeling that he only stood up to show me how big he was. Almost as big as the butler, but with more stomach, and his hair was gray. He really looked like a man who owned half a city and the people in it and had done the things you have to do to get to own them.

I sat down in the chair and put my hat on my knees. He eased down and swiveled back in his chair. There was a big cigar box on the desk. It stood five or six inches high on little round knobs and it was covered with fancy carving. He pushed it across the desk toward me with the point of a brass letter opener. I shook my head.

"What did you want to see me about?"

He took his time. I guess he had always been smart enough to take his time answering questions. When he did speak it came fast and sharp with a hard edge on it.

"Let's get the haggling done with," he said. "I'm a rich man. Nobody works for me for pennies."

"I wasn't worried about it," I said. "What did you want me to do?"

He waited again. I knew he wasn't used to being pushed. So I pushed him.

"I'm still talking about money," he said. "After we get through with that we'll talk about the work."

I shook my head, stood up.

He kept on trying. "Say one thousand retainer and five hundred a week, including local expenses?"

He had a checkbook there and a heavy gold fountain pen in his hand. My breath stopped for only half a second, not long enough for him to notice. My average weekly take is never anything like five hundred bucks.

"This is just a matter of routine, Mr. Warfield," I said. "There are jobs I can't do. I don't know which ones they are till I hear about them. I think things out better when my hands are not wrapped up in a lot of money."

6

He moved his head up away from the checkbook into the shadow again, but I could feel his eyes going over me. He reached for the cigar box, flicked the cover up. I saw a row of handsomely wrapped stogies. He got one out, clipped the end of it, put it in his mouth and lit up. He blew a long thin cloud of smoke.

"Sit down," he said.

After an interval I sat down.

"A couple of weeks ago," he said, "my wife walked out on me."

There was no expression in the way he said it. And by itself it meant nothing to me. It was only number one in a list of facts.

"She's living alone in an apartment on the sixth floor of the Amberley Apartments on Sheridan Road," he said, "and she's in danger. I want you to watch her. I wouldn't want any harm to come to her."

I looked at him across the white glow on top of the desk. "What kind of danger?"

He shrugged. "Maybe a snatch. Something. There've been threats."

"Letters?"

"By telephone."

"You've told her about it?"

There was another of his pauses—a long one. "Right at the present time," he said slowly, "we're not speaking."

"And you wouldn't want her to know you'd hired her a bodyguard."

"She wouldn't go for it. You'll have to act without her knowing."

It was my turn to pause—not too long—just long enough. He was reaching for that pen again.

"And report back to you, of course—on her movements?"

"As a check on you," he said, "—naturally."

"As a check on me."

He waited with the pen poised over the checkbook. With his face down in the light he looked gray all over and flabby under the eyes. His chin was still clean and hard, but the little sacs were forming here and there. And his thick lips were a little slack.

I twirled my hat once around my finger, grabbed it before it fell and stood up again.

"I can't take it on," I said. "It's not my kind of job. If you just picked my name out of the book, you wouldn't necessarily know that. Sorry I took up your time."

He didn't say anything. He folded the checkbook and dropped it into the top drawer of the desk. He dropped the pen in after it and closed the drawer silently.

"Good night," I said.

I walked across the room toward the door with my back to him, ambling, as when I had come in. It came home to me then, the meaning of that crack he'd made about how much farther it was "going out," than "coming in." Some trick in the lighting, something about the pattern of the door, made it seem small and far off. And the floor was heavily carpeted, so that your steps made no sound. You couldn't hear yourself walking and I imagined that if you were scared and looked at that door, trying to get out in a hurry without showing the fear, you would wonder whether you were walking at all.

It came as I reached for the doorknob—a tiny rush of wind past my cheek, followed half a watch tick later by the splintering thud of steel going into wood and then the faintest tingle of vibration as the handle shuddered there in the doorjamb beside my head.

I was close enough so that it could have looked as if I had just gone ahead and reached for the knob to open the door, instead of grabbing the handiest thing by which to steady myself—long enough anyway to keep from looking back.

The next part of it was strictly theater, which ordinarily I don't go in for. But he had me riled.

I dropped the doorknob, straightened up, pulled the knife out of the wall and weighed it. Then I let him have it back, fast and hard, right into that beautiful walnut cigar box near his left hand. It was a better shot than I had hoped for. It went in clean and the box barely moved on the polished desk top. I don't know whether it impressed him. Probably not.

I opened the door and went out without looking at him again. The big butler appeared from nowhere in the middle of the reception hall, walked to the front door and let me out. I stopped for a minute, looking at him. He looked back at me without expression. He was ugly enough, with his smashed nose, too frequently reset jaw and cauliflower ears, to scare the daylights out of anybody.

"I've seen you before," I said. "Long before."

"Not me, sir," he said, nearly strangling on the "sir."

"Yes, sir. You, sir," I said. "You fought Tony Peccati in 1929. I remember. They carried you out after the third round. You stood there and let him hit you."

It wasn't anything he wanted to remember. He kept still.

"Who had the dough on Peccati?" I asked. I jerked my head back toward the library. "Him?"

"Good night," he said.

"All right. But he can't give you your jaw back, and your smeller."

He pushed the door to slowly, pushing me outside. I stood there for a minute trying to remember his name, then I went down the wide steps and across the asphalt to my car.

There was a girl in it. A girl in a fur coat, with red hair. A good-looking girl. I opened the door and slid under the wheel. I waited a while, but she just sat there. Finally I took a chance and asked her a question.

"What are you selling?"

She stuck a cigarette in her mouth and flicked a gold lighter. She turned her face to me, holding the light so I could see her.

"Don't you know me?" she said. "Or is my publicity falling off?"

"Yeah," I said, tired of the game. "You sing at the Mobile. Or maybe you dance. I never go there. Your name is Marilyn Mayfair."

"I sing and dance. Of course, Marilyn Mayfair isn't my real name."

"No kidding."

"What's your name?"

"People call me Mac."

"All right, Mac. Let's go."

"You're Warfield's current playmate."

She pouted. "Let's not be crude. Let's say I'm a friend of the family."

"All right. What do you want?"

"Want a lift. My car's in the garage with a cold in the carburetor. You take me to the Drive and I'll get a cab."

I started the car. We made the trip in silence till we got to the gate.

He had the place fenced like the yard at Joliet. This high stone wall, six feet thick, went all the way along the front and back on both sides of the estate, to the edge of the bluff that dropped straight down to the lake. He had a private little harbor back there and rumor said he had it mined to keep anyone from coming in that way unannounced. I doubted the rumors. There were nothing but rocks along the shore. His own yacht was moored well out and guarded the channel into the harbor. This iron gate between the stone pillars was the only entrance.

When you came in you stopped at the gate and rang a bell. There was a telephone there hanging on the side of the pillar and after a while a voice would answer and when you gave your name, if you were somebody he wanted to see, a big buzzing would start and the gates would swing open slowly. They started to close as you drove through and barely missed clipping your back bumper if you loitered. Going out you went through the same procedure.

I sat there for a minute. "Haven't you got a key?" I asked.

She laughed. "There are two keys. He has one and his wife has the other."

"His wife still has it?"

She shrugged. "I wouldn't know."

I climbed out of the car and went to the telephone. There were bushes along the drive and near the gate. The sprinkling system had been turned off as I left the house and the dripping shrubbery slapped against my coat. I rang the bell and heard the voice of his butler. I said my name and he hung up. That buzzing started and I jumped back into the car and roared out of the place, onto the street.

"Where did you want to go?" I asked.

She laughed again. "I know a hundred men who would beg for the privilege of taking me all over town—alone in a car like this—"

"I've been sick," I said.

She laughed. "You're a private detective, aren't you?"

"How did you guess?"

"I don't know. You look rugged, like a real man, someone a girl could really latch onto."

"Cut it out."

"What are you going to do for him?" she gestured backward with her thumb.

"Maybe you could catch a cab along in here. There's a big intersection just ahead."

She laughed some more. It was a gay, professional laugh. It wasn't unpleasant, nor was it exactly real.

"Some night," she said, "when I have time I'm going to come over and see you. I'd like to find out how thick that shell really is."

"Like the hide of a rhinoceros," I said.

"Did he throw that knife at you?" she asked. "He does that to everybody the first time he meets them. It's his idea of a joke. He did it to me the first night I came out here. I'm telling you—I held on; I didn't scream. I didn't drop dead. But—I'm telling you…"

I stopped for a light. There was a business corner, with some cabs parked along the curb next to us. She opened the door.

"All right, Mac," she said. "If you're going to push me. Thanks for the lift."

She ducked into a cab while I was still waiting for the light. I heard her tell the driver: "The Mobile Club, in a hurry."

The cab drew away and I moved when the light changed a moment later. She'd been heavily perfumed and I opened both windows to air the car out. I don't hate women, generally speaking. But I don't go for that forward type.

CHAPTER 2

By the time I got back to my office and rooms on the near North Side, I had begun to wonder just how much it was worth—the honor of being one of possibly two or three things Warfield had been unable to buy in his lifetime. As a matter of cold cash, it was worth exactly nothing. On the other hand, I still had my pride. I would remind myself to eat some of it for breakfast.

I locked the car, crossed the street to Jerry's place, picked up a late paper and ate a ham sandwich and a glass of milk. Then I went back across the street, climbed the six steps to the vestibule, went into the hall and stuck my key in the door of Apartment 1. The lock stuck and I had to play with it to tumble it open. I slid my hand along the wall, found the light switch and prodded. Then I stood there in the doorway, blinking.

There were two of them, nicely built, clean-shaven chaps, all dressed up in black coats and hats. One of them leaned against my desk with his arms folded. The other one, a fat lad, leaned against the mantel over the fake fireplace, smoking a cigar. There wasn't an expression in their faces. There never is.

I stood there slapping my newspaper against my knee. I looked first at one of them, then at the other. Then I looked back over my shoulder.

The third one came slowly toward the front of the building, out of the shadows at the end of the hall. He looked like the other two, more or less. He kept coming till he stood directly behind me. There was a pause and then he put his hand in the middle of my back and pushed, very gently. I walked in and he followed me, closing the door behind us. After he'd closed it he leaned against it, facing the room.

I dropped my hat and newspaper on the desk and sat down in the swivel chair.

"All right," I said. "Tell me a story."

After a long time the one who had been leaning against my desk moved. He turned, gracefully, all in one easy motion, like a cat, until he had made a half turn, so that instead of leaning on his behind, facing the door, he was leaning on his gloved hands, facing me.

It was an interesting face: white, smooth and very well cared for. There was something wrong with his nose. Not much. Just a tiny little something that you would notice only if you were studying him, as I was, out of habit—in order never to forget. A faint line, a shade whiter than the rest of his face, beginning in the corner of his left eye and running down beside his nose, almost, not quite, to his upper lip. It made his nose look a little off-center. Not crooked enough to bother anybody. Just enough to remember. His eyes I didn't notice. There was nothing-special about them. They all have the same kind of eyes. Flat.

I didn't know who they were. There are a lot of them around.

"You been out to see Warfield," he said.

His voice and his lips said two different things at the same time.

We both waited. I waited longer.

"You left here at 7:45. You bought a paper in Evanston. You got to Warfield's at 8:45. You called up from the gate and they opened it. You drove up to the house, rang the bell and the butler let you in. You stayed there fifteen minutes. You came out and that girl of his was in the car. You drove down the drive to the road. You let the girl out at the Walgreen Drugstore a mile down the road. You got back here at 9:42, went across the street and ate a sandwich. It was a ham sandwich with mustard and lettuce. Then you came in here."

I waited some more.

"So we know that," he said.

"All right," I said. "That's what you know."

He was very patient, quiet and slow talking. He would always be quiet and slow, but he would not always be patient.

"So what we got to know beside that is why you went to Warfield and what you are supposed to do for him. Nothing personal. We just got to get that information."

"For whom?"

"For a guy," he said.

I studied him some more. I didn't learn anything.

"You know better than that," I said. "Maybe you can get the dope from Warfield."

The single shift of his eyes showed me his patience had run out. There was a hand in my hair, pulling my head back so that the skin stretched taut across my throat. Looking up and back I saw the chin and the hat brim of the lad who had been leaning against the fireplace. Sticking out from somewhere between the chin and the hat was a thick cigar. It wasn't much to look at, but right then I couldn't look anywhere else.

Something cold and thin lay suddenly against the side of my neck, just under my chin. The hand in my hair tightened.

Three minutes went by.

"Want to say something?" a voice asked.

"Uh-huh." My Adam's apple didn't move.

The cold thing went away and the hand in my hair loosened enough so I could straighten my head. The man with the crooked nose still leaned on his hands across from me, where he had always been.

"Warfield gave you something," he said. "Where is it?"

I just looked at him. "Tell him to get his hand out of my hair," I said.

His eyes shifted and the hand went away.

"He didn't give me anything," I said, "and I don't know where anything is."

"You could maybe still have it in your car," he said. "Or you could have dropped it off on your way back—or you could have left it across the street in that bar. All we want to know—what did you do with it?"

I tried sincerity. "This is the God's truth." I said, "though I don't know why I make the effort: Warfield gave me nothing. I did not bring anything away from there. I don't know what you're looking for."

He straightened away from the desk and studied me. He kept hitting his gloved left fist into the palm of his right hand, gently, without making a sound.

I was fed up with the whole batch of them—Warfield and his wife and these night crawlers, too. I had not made any money on Warfield, I was not making any on these mugs and I would not be able to make any the next day if I didn't get some sleep. I stood up.

"My office is closed," I said. "You're welcome to stay here all night if you want to. I'm going to bed."

I reached across the desk and switched off the lamp. It was only a gesture. The ceiling light was still on. I was just playing busy executive.

The man with the crooked nose said, "No. You got to come with us. Maybe you're on the level. I don't know. I don't make those decisions."

"Some other time," I said. "Tonight I'm sleepy."

I walked around the front of the desk past Crooked Nose and back toward the rear door that led to my living quarters. Nobody moved except me, until I reached for the door. Then the ceiling light went out and that one with the cigar was behind me—close—with one hand on my twisted wrist and the other clamped against my mouth.

He didn't realize what he was doing. I have very strong teeth. I snapped, caught his little finger just above the knuckle and chewed on it. He didn't give me a chance to get to the bone. While he was trying to shake it free of my teeth I broke his wrist lock, turned and hit him three times as hard as I could, as low as I could.

He had plenty of control. He didn't holler when I bit him, nor scream when I socked his belly. He just grunted once and caved in at the knees. He grabbed my throat as he sagged, trying to pull me down with him, but

I shook him off and went across the room fast, wondering what the other two were doing.

The other two were doing all right. One of them was waiting for me. I walked into his arms and he pushed my shoulder, turning me, and shoved a hard, round little thing into my ribs.

The other one came up close. Something rattled. He grabbed my left wrist, snapped a steel band around it and reached for my right wrist. I threw the right wrist at his face. The guy in back tapped me behind the ear —just hard enough to blind me for the time it took to get the cuffs on both my wrists.

"What about Al?" said the one behind me.

"Leave him lay," Crooked Nose said. "He knows the way home."

Crooked Nose walked away and the gun in my ribs prodded me after him. He stopped short at the door and I ran into him, bumping my nose against his shoulder. He didn't like that. He turned and looked me full in the face. Then he lifted his hand and gave me the back of it across my mouth. I licked my lips to keep the blood from dribbling down over my chin.

He opened the door, glanced into the dimly lit hall and then walked to the outer door. The gun jabbed my ribs and I followed. Outside the three of us strolled casually down the steps. Across the street Jerry's place was still lighted up. But business was slack. Nobody was going in—or coming out.

A big Buick sedan was parked at the curb a little way down the street toward the Boulevard. We walked that way, diagonally across the sidewalk.

We hadn't quite reached the car when this big figure hove in sight—a giant in black clothes walking toward us along the sidewalk. A package swung from one hand beside him. He was looking up at the house numbers, walking slowly, and didn't see us. But we saw him. Crooked Nose saw him and stopped.

"Lefty!" he said. It was a dull, whispered command.

The boy with the gun stepped a little way out from behind me and shot the giant three times in the stomach. The big man leaned forward, holding the package tight against himself. Then he fell, slowly and full length with a great thud, like a tree.

"The package!" Crooked Nose whispered and Lefty ran across the walk to the crumpled-up giant.

A window went up in my building.

Crooked Nose swung around and crowded me against the side of the car. He put his gloved hand on my throat and pushed.

14

I heard a whistle blow down the street and running steps and knew it was Pete Barbella on his beat. I kicked Crooked Nose in the shin and buried my linked hands in his belly. It was my turn next anyway. I had nothing to lose. He swung me away from the car and called, "Cops, Lefty!"

The motor roared, the door slammed and the big car was gone before Pete had got his holster opened. But the big guy still lay there on the sidewalk. Some people came warily across from Jerry's place and heads were leaning out of windows along the street.

Pete Barbella panted into my face. "Who was it?"

"I don't know, Pete," I said. "Send one of these people for a doctor and help me get him in the office."

"I'll do the shoving," Pete said, doing it, and while he was doing it I went over to the guy on the sidewalk. The cuffs bit into my wrists as I pushed him over far enough to get a look at his face. The package was still there and after I saw his face I snaked it out from under him and dropped it behind the low hedge running along the walk.

Pete Barbella came over. "Who is he?" he asked, as if I ought to know everything.

"Warfield's butler."

"Warfield? No!"

"Yeah."

The big boy's lips were moving. I leaned over him and listened. He worked at it a long time and finally I heard him wheeze: "...a safe place..."

Pete hadn't heard it.

"Better move him inside," he said.

"Better not," I said. "I just remembered something."

I straightened and ran up the steps to my building, wishing for the bracelets to drop off, which they didn't. The blonde who lived on the third floor was standing in the vestibule and she screamed when I busted in, then recognized me gratefully.

"Get back out of the way," I said.

She went up a few steps and sat down. My key was still in the lock and I twisted it and pushed the door open with my foot. I waited, heard nothing, reached around the edge of the jamb and found the switch. I blinked at the light, then searched the room from outside before I went in. It was empty and I went in and looked around. It was still empty. I opened the door to my living quarters, lighted them up and looked everywhere, including the shower. Nobody there.

When I came out of the bedroom the blonde was standing in the office door.

"I heard the back door slam just as I came downstairs," she said. "Just a couple of minutes before you came in." I ran past her to the back door, into the areaway and on to the alley behind the street. It was awkward running with my hands tied up in front that way. Then I went back to the office. With two minutes' start he could be in the Loop by now.

"What happened?" the blonde asked.

I picked up the telephone with both hands and laid it on the desk. Then I dialed.

"A man just died."

"Who?"

"I don't know."

I finished dialing and held the phone up with both hands.

"Why don't you take those off?" she asked.

"Why don't you go to bed?" I said.

"Good night," she said. "God forbid I should ever again rent an apartment in the same house with a private cop."

She went away.

Homicide came on and Donovan was in.

"Come on over," I told him. "We're having a little party."

"What should I bring?"

"A camera and the coroner."

He hung up. I was glad he'd been on duty. I was always glad when it could be Donovan.

CHAPTER 3

Donovan made a lot of smart cracks while he took my handcuffs off with a little gadget whose secret he would never let me in on and we sat around my office after everybody had gone.

Donovan said, "The butler's name was Alex. Used to be a fighter. He did a stretch once for pandering and Warfield sprung him. I remember those things. Why would he be coming to you? You turned down Warfield's job—whatever it was."

"I don't know that he was coming to me."

"Must have been."

"All right."

"Describe those hoods again."

I did it, in the best detail I could, while Donovan sat hunched over in the chair, poker-faced, searching his memory. When I finished he said, "The fat one don't ring a bell and the one called Lefty don't mean a thing to me. The one with the nose—him I think I saw some place. But I'm not sure. I'll look around. You want to come?"

"No thanks," I said. "Got a heavy engagement."

Donovan got up. "I wish you would go into some other line of work," he said. "You make me nervous."

"I'm all right. If I need you, I'll holler."

"So-long," he said, going out, his squat, wide frame filling the door.

As always, I was sorry to see him go. He was like a father. The best cop in town, the one who had trained me and the one who raised the most hell when they pushed me off the force—when Warfield was still Scarpone and didn't own quite so much of the town. But enough at that.

But he had to go and I had some work of my own.

I gave him five minutes, then went outside, down the steps and up the walk to that spot where the butler had died and where I had dropped his package behind the hedge. It was still there and I picked it up and carried it back to the office.

It was about twelve inches by sixteen and three or four inches thick. It wasn't heavy. Under the brown wrapping paper was another layer of wrapping paper. It was sealed tight all around. Across the top of this lay a plain white No. 10 envelope, with my name on it. I ripped the envelope off and opened it. There was a piece of note paper and a check. On the note paper it said:

The thing in this package belongs to my wife, who is a fool. Like you. But I can trust you. I will leave my entire estate to my wife, and this too. But if I leave this thing lay around here, somebody will steal it after I die before she gets it.

I pay you to take it to her.

So I'm a fool too. Like everybody else.

* * * *

The check was for two hundred dollars. I put it in my pocket, thinking about how you couldn't buy life for Warfield's dead competition for that money. It was not up to me to decide whether the competition was better off dead.

I went into the bathroom, washed my face and hands and changed my tie. I picked up the package from my desk, turned out the lights and went outside. It was cold now. I hadn't noticed this before. I went back and got my coat.

I drove slowly out the Boulevard, got onto Sheridan Road and went four or five miles, out around the Edge-water Beach.

The Amberley Apartments were white stone with plenty of wrought iron grille work around the windows and on the heavy front door. I pushed through it, carrying the package, and scanned the names under the brass boxes set in the marble walls of the vestibule. Mrs. Cynthia Warfield was in Number 617. I went up three steps and tried the door into the foyer. It was locked. It was the kind that would always be locked after 11 p.m. You had to have a key or the right name. I didn't know any names except Scarpone, Warfield and my own and I had a hunch she wouldn't open for any of them.

I waited a couple of minutes, but nobody showed up. I couldn't wait all night. I stabbed the ivory button under her name and put my ear to the speaking tube. I got nothing but silence. I leaned on it some more.

The street door opened and a woman came into the vestibule. Fast. She was dressed expensively, she carried a long, narrow suitcase, she was fairly beautiful and she did not glance at me or waste any time getting from the street door across the vestibule and up the steps to the locked door that led to the foyer. She wasn't exactly running, but she was moving the way well-bred ladies move when they are trying to get somewhere in a hurry.

I pulled the door open for her after she had it unlocked.

"Lucky me," I said. "I forgot my key. Good thing you came in. Hate to spend the night out here."

She looked at me over her shoulder and her eyes were startled for a moment, then under control again right away. She stepped into the foyer and I followed her to the automatic elevator.

It was up at the top. She rang for it and we stood there, the way people do who live in the same house and never speak to one another, looking in different directions, never quite meeting a gaze head on and still trying not to appear unfriendly. One of the most complicated maneuvers of urban life.

There were seven floors. She pushed the button for the sixth and I pushed the seventh. Whoever she was, I didn't want her to get suspicious in the elevator. You can raise hell in an elevator, just by pushing buttons.

At the sixth floor I pushed back the grating and held the outer door while she stepped out. Then I let them close, rode to the seventh and got out. I walked along the carpeted hall toward the back to the service stairs. I went down to the sixth floor and back along the hall to No. 617. There was a light underneath the door.

I tapped the brass knocker lightly. After a moment a woman's voice said, "Yes?"

I knocked again. I counted to twenty-five before the door opened.

This time she was more than startled. She was scared. The fear flared in her eyes and you could see the fight she put up to clear it out. Most of it went away.

"What do you want?"

"You're Mrs. Warfield?" I asked.

"Who are you?"

I gave her my card. She looked at it, frowned, gave it back to me. "I don't recall sending for you."

"You didn't. I think you'll want to talk to me though. I have something for you."

She hesitated a long time. She looked back into the room, then back at me. The thought in her head was just a cloud at first, then it cleared and squeezed into her eyes full force. For some reason she had decided I looked good to her. "Come in," she said, and stepped back into the room.

I went in and she closed the door. She had thrown her coat down on a davenport and I sat down beside it. There was a coffee table there with a bottle of Scotch and some glasses. She leaned over and poured one. She looked at me and I shook my head. She took the drink straight and crossed the room to sit in a straight chair facing me.

Her face was the type usually described as patrician. She had brown hair, casually dressed, fine straight features, with full lips and gray eyes. She was thirty-one, maybe thirty-two. She did not look happy. She looked as if she had been very unhappy for a long, long time. I could not imagine her with Warfield and I could not imagine her a fool.

I laid the package on the coffee table.

"Your husband asked me to bring you this."

Her voice was far off and quite cold. "You're employed by him?"

"Not any more. I was until a moment ago. Now I'm—at liberty."

After a moment she said, "How interesting. Possibly you could spend your free time to better advantage than by sitting around here."

"Possibly," I said, without moving.

She yawned.

"Don't work so hard on it, Mrs. Warfield."

"I beg your pardon?"

"Frankly—I'm hanging around thinking maybe I can sell my services. I understand you're in some personal danger."

"I?" she said, as if it were ridiculous.

"I didn't think much of it myself, at first. Now I'm not so sure. You're upset at the moment. I don't know why."

She didn't explain why.

"You thought I might want to hire a bodyguard?"

"The thought entered my head. We've got to live."

"Is it common practice in your profession—to solicit business directly like this?"

"No. But once in a while, playing a hunch, a cop might try to put himself in the way of something."

She finished her drink.

"You're not saying very much," she said. "Who told you I'm in danger?"

"Are you in danger?"

She looked into her glass, turned it over and over in her fingers. "I don't know."

I let her think about it for a while. The control she had shown at first was slipping a little. She sat with one knee crossed over the other and the point of her toe kept twitching, pointing first one way, then the other. But that was the only sign.

She looked up suddenly. "How do I check on you? How do I know I can trust you?"

"That's fair enough. You could call Lieutenant Donovan, homicide squad. He's known me a long time. He's a man tells the truth."

Her toe stopped twitching, hung absolutely motionless.

"Why did you say that?"

"I was only giving you a reference."

20

She went back to staring at her glass. "Donovan. I seem to have heard of him. He has a good name."

"Best there is."

"I won't call him. If you're willing to name him, I'll take your word for it. I might call him later." She came over and poured some more whisky into her glass. The hand that held it was shaking. "That is," she said, looking straight into my eyes, "if I decide to hire you."

"Do you always drink like this?" I asked.

She didn't answer. She had gone back to her chair. She sat now with the glass in her two hands in her lap, her ankles crossed and tucked back under the chair.

"How much would it cost?" she said. "To hire you?"

"Depends," I said. "If you just want me to go along when you go out, it's by the hour. Five dollars an hour, plus lunch money, theater tickets, etc. If you want me around all the time—I move in here, sleep on the couch or in the spare bedroom, never leave you alone, then it's by the day. Twenty dollars a day."

She twisted her head to look out the window. "Ridiculous," she said under her breath.

"It's the best rate I can offer."

"I didn't mean that." She didn't explain what she did mean.

"Why did you leave your husband, Mrs. Warfield?"

Her head jerked around. "I beg your pardon?"

"If you don't like that one, here's another. Why did you sic those professional sluggers onto me?"

"I don't understand."

"Tonight. They dropped in for tea a couple of hours ago. Knew an awful lot about my movements. Kept asking questions. Got a little rough about it. They finally went away. They wanted me to go along. And I would have. Only just about then Warfield's butler came down the street and they shot him. Three times."

"Alex?"

"If that's his name."

"They shot Alex?"

"They didn't buy him a drink. The point of this story is that at the time of the shooting Alex was carrying this package."

She wasn't so cocky now. "But—why?"

"I don't know. Maybe you know."

"I don't even know who they were. You think I hired some men to get information from you?"

"Somebody hired them. They don't work free."

"Really—I think we're wasting time. Obviously you're only trying to frighten me."

"You were already frightened. I only want to know why. You could be frightened because you did hire these gorillas and when you found they'd killed Alex, you were afraid you'd be held as an accessory. But I doubt that now."

"How big of you."

I got up. I walked over to her chair and stood there with my feet apart and my hands in my pockets, like a tough cop, and gave her some of that bullying technique. So far I had liked her. I wanted to go on liking her.

"You can stop being snotty, Mrs. Warfield. I've been to a lot of trouble tonight and most of it was unpleasant. You can throw me out if you want to. It's your life. Only—I brought you this package, for money. On account of this package somebody is already dead. I don't want to read in tomorrow's paper that you're dead, too."

She got up, slid past me, crossed the room to the coffee table and picked up the package. She found a letter opener, sat down on the davenport and slit the brown paper around the edges. Inside there was a box. She lifted the lid off the box.

It was a book—an old book. I could tell that from the binding. She didn't open it and I couldn't see what it was about.

One of her hands went to her throat. She stared at me. "From—him?"

"That's right."

"He paid you to bring this to me?"

"He did."

Her face was contorted with the struggle between disbelief and obvious fact. She stared at me, at the book, at me again. Then she began to laugh. Slow and quiet at first, then louder, until she was trembling with the violence of it. It went on for quite a while and I let it go. I went back to the davenport and sat down beside her. Finally she quieted some, tried to speak and couldn't. She put her forehead down on her crossed hands on the arm of the davenport and I didn't know whether she was laughing now or crying. When she spoke it came in little gasps with wide spaces of time between the words.

"He—did this? He paid you—to bring me this book? He—Warfield—did this?"

She paused to catch her breath.

"Oh, solicitude! Oh, how lovely! What a wrong I've done him!"

She got out of her chair, picked up the glass and leaned over the coffee table, lurching a little, as if she were drunk. But I knew she wasn't.

It wouldn't be long though. She poured out half a glass. I took it out of her hand, poured most of it out into another glass on the table and gave the rest back to her. She stood there like a baby and let me do it. Then she found her way across the room to the chair and sank into it.

"How long have you been married to him?" I asked.

"Ten years." Her voice was all gone now, tired and hollow and distant. "Ten long, repulsive years. My father sold me to him twenty years ago—for a million dollars and a guaranteed reputation. Reputation. One of the oldest families in town, honorable to the last bastion.

"They let me live ten years without knowing what it was about—what anything was about. They sent me to an Eastern finishing school to learn about the birds and bees. I never read the newspapers, I never went to the movies. I learned how to behave with dignity, how to speak correctly, how to seat guests at a table. I went to Europe and visited the ruins.

"When I came home from school the time was up. They told me I was going to marry Warfield. I said I didn't want to. They said that if I didn't my father would go to jail, my mother would be without a cent and I would have to go to work in the five-and-ten-cent store. I didn't know anything about Warfield. I just didn't like him. I thought a girl married someone nearer her own age, someone who liked the same things she did.

"But they drew a horrible picture. I didn't understand it, but I didn't want to see my father go to jail. I married Warfield."

She took a swallow from her glass, looked at the bottle and looked away. She got up and walked to the window and stood looking out. After a while she turned and came back across the room. She stood there, a little unsteady for a moment, then she straightened and went through that wonderful reorganization again that made her look like what they'd trained her to be.

I held out her coat. She looked at it without understanding.

"We're going to look something up, for the record," I said. "All I can say is that you talk too much, and most of it is in the wrong tense."

She slid into the coat. Her mouth was shut tight now. She didn't say a word as we turned off the lights, went out and got into the elevator. She didn't say anything until we had got into the car and were headed out the Drive going north, and then she spoke only because I asked her a question.

"What's that book?"

"What book?"

"The one I brought you."

"Oh... An original Gutenberg Bible, printed in 1455. It's been in my family for years. I think it's quite valuable."

"How valuable, in money?"

"Perhaps fifty thousand dollars. This is only one of two volumes. The other was destroyed in the Fire."

"Some book."

"Not enough to kill a man for."

"No. Not unless you're awfully hungry."

I drove fast along the Drive. It was nearly 2 a.m. and the traffic was light. She sat hunched down by the door on her side, the collar of her coat high around her neck.

"Where are we going?" she asked after a while.

"We're going to annoy the cops a little—if it isn't too late."

I pulled up in front of the iron gate. She looked at me wide-eyed.

"I should have guessed," she said.

"You have a key?"

"Yes."

"Let's have it."

She dug around in her purse and came up with a small key.

"It's the little black door in the pillar," she said. "Open it and push the button inside."

I climbed out and went to the pillar. There was a little black door. I put the key in, twisted and the door swung open. I reached inside, groping for a button. Something clicked and that buzzing started. The gates swung back slowly. I ran back to the car, squeezed through just in time. The gates swung to behind us with a clatter.

It was very foggy now and my lights were yellow blobs searching for the winding drive. A couple of times I got off and felt my tires sinking into the soft green lawn. The house itself was hidden and only loomed gray and cold ahead of us after I'd traveled what seemed like an hour. There was a dim light in the portico and I stopped directly in front of it. Then I thought better of it, started up again and slid on a way into the fog.

I got out on my side, went around to open her door. She started to climb out, then changed her mind and sat back. "I'm not going in. I'll wait."

"Nothing to be afraid of."

"I'll wait."

I didn't have time to argue. It wasn't important anyway. It was only that I was afraid to leave her out of my sight.

I ran up the steps to the front door. It was locked. I went back to the car, got her key and returned to open the door. There was a dim light in the reception hall and a light showing under the door of the library. Nobody was about.

I crossed the reception hall quickly. The library door was unlocked. I twisted the knob and pushed it open. The lamp on Warfield's desk was burning. Warfield wasn't in sight. In the white glow of the lamp I saw the polished top of the desk—but no walnut cigar box—no knife.

24

I went across the library to the desk. Warfield's chair lay on its back, as if he had tipped back in it a little too far and the castors had slipped out from under him. I went around the desk.

Something had certainly slipped out from under him. Warfield was lying on his back too, his feet under the desk, his arms outstretched. And sticking straight up out of his chest was that knife, the one he'd thrown at me, the one I'd thrown back at him.

I guess that hadn't been enough. Because he'd been beaten considerably too. He had practically nothing left in the way of a face and that little didn't make much sense.

I felt one of his hands. It was cold, but just barely. He'd been alive within the last three hours.

I looked around where he was. There wasn't much. There wasn't anything he could have been beaten with. There was a lot of blood around where the knife had gone in and it looked well placed. So I couldn't see why he had been beaten too. He must have been pretty dead already.

I walked away from Warfield, across the room to the fireplace. The desk lamp didn't carry that far and I struck a match to light it up. It was a big fireplace—big enough for a six-foot log—with a heavy oak mantel. At one side of the firebox was a brass standard, a couple of feet high with three loops for tools. Resting snugly in one loop was a pair of tongs, bright, polished brass, with a lion's head for handle. In the second loop was a little shovel, also with lion's head. In the third loop, where there ought to have been a poker, there wasn't anything at all. I looked around that part of the room, but there wasn't any poker anywhere. Nor anything else.

I went outside, closing the library door behind me, crossed the reception hall to the front door, went out and down the steps, and crossed the drive to the car.

She just sat there while I got away from the place onto the street and well on the way back to town. I let her sit. If anything was going to come out, I wanted it to come out straight and short. We didn't have very long to go over it.

She chewed up the edges of a hankie, stared out the window and after a while she began to talk.

"He was a pig. He was a pig in everything he did. We had a whole harem in that house. He was very discreet about it. We kept getting new servants all the time, girls. They were always pretty and round and careless of their talk. They didn't work. They just hung around. I didn't know at first—I didn't know anything. When I learned, it didn't really matter any more.

"He didn't bother me much after the first year. I found out how to avoid him."

She was in bad shape. She was a trained patrician, who had kept all this bottled up for ten years and it was rough coming out. She was doing a lot of retching over it.

"The last one he had," she said, "was this Mayfair person. She threw everybody else out, got him all to herself."

"Threw you out, too?"

"Don't be insulting."

"I didn't mean to be."

"I understand he planned to leave everything to her. He had a lot to leave."

"What time did you go out there?"

"About eleven-thirty."

"You checked your car out of the apartment garage to make the trip?"

"I'd been out for several hours. I had the car. There were some things I'd left behind and I wanted to pick them up."

"You put the car away when you came back?"

"I stopped at the garage door. The attendant came and got it."

"You stop anywhere out around there?"

"At a filling station about half a mile from the house."

"They know you?"

"I was a regular customer."

"That was on your way out or your way back?"

"On the way out."

"That's fine."

I was getting back into the city and I slowed down.

"How long were you there?"

"Maybe half an hour, in my room, going through my things."

"Aren't there any servants in that house?"

"I had a personal maid who was dismissed when I left. Two weeks ago. There was a small staff—a couple of cleaning women, a cook, a gardener. They lived in a little house on the back corner of the estate. Alex was the only one who stayed in the big house all the time."

"They had all gone to bed when you got out there?"

"Either to bed or out. I didn't see Alex around."

"Alex was getting himself shot in the stomach."

She stuffed the handkerchief in her mouth. I slid past the Drake Hotel, turned onto the Avenue and headed for the Water Tower.

"All right," I said, "get set. Get hold of yourself, because the one that's coming up is the big one, the only one I'll have to go on."

26

She took the handkerchief out and straightened a little in her seat. She stared straight ahead through the windshield.

"Did you do it?"

I waited for the light at Chicago Avenue, drove slowly to my street, stopped for the left turn, gave the signal, made the turn and was halfway down the block before it came.

"No."

"That will help a little," I said. "I don't know why I believe you. You'd have guts enough to do it if you felt you had to."

She kept quiet.

"How did you happen to run onto him?"

"It was an accident. I packed what I'd come for and went downstairs to the reception hall. I looked for Alex. I wanted to open the gate from the house and I wanted to tell him so he could close it after I'd gone out. I didn't find him. I pushed the button to open the gate. Then I noticed the library door was ajar. The light was on and I glanced in. Warfield wasn't at his desk. I thought Alex might be in the library so I went in. It was unusual for the desk light to be on when my—husband—wasn't there. I went to the desk."

She chewed some more of the hankie.

"I ran out. For some reason I pulled the library door shut as I went. I drove away as fast as I could, drove to the apartment. You know the rest."

It was no good, of course. True maybe, but no good, if she had really been all alone.

"When you drove out," I said, "you didn't stop to close the gate?"

"I didn't think about it. I'd have been afraid to stop."

"Mn-hmn. Wonder who closed it?"

"Not necessarily anyone. It's on some sort of timing device. It closes automatically after five minutes."

"Oh."

I left her in the car, went up the steps into the building and opened my door. I didn't have any visitors in the office. I went to the bedroom and kitchen and looked them over and then back to the car.

"Come on."

"Where are we now?" she said. There was nothing left in her voice except the roughness of exhaustion.

"At my place. We're lucky. For a change everybody around here went to bed early."

I helped her out of the car and steadied her up the steps into the office. I steered her back through the office into the bedroom, pushed her into a chair and hunted up some brandy. I poured a stiff shot for her, started to put it away, then decided to take one myself. It tasted good.

I closed and locked the door between the bedroom and the office, checked to see that all the blinds in this part of my rooms were drawn and snapped on a lamp. I sat down on the studio couch which is my bed and tried to think some more.

"I can't stay here," she said.

I was thinking about something else.

"They won't look for you here right away. They won't connect us for a few hours, until they get the Alex shooting tied up with it. Their first conclusion will be it's the same crowd. Then they'll find you were out there at the right time. After that they'll think of nobody but you."

"But, I mean—I—" Then I caught on.

"My God! The birds and the bees—that really is all they ever taught you, isn't it?"

"Please don't—"

"Look, Mrs. Warfield. You can't afford the luxury of automatic reactions right now. You're the woman who murdered her husband. You not only murdered him. You smashed his face in. They're going to have you standing in a cell screaming at the reporters: 'Yes, I killed him! And I'm glad, glad, glad! You understand! GLAD!"

"I didn't—I didn't touch him—I—"

"That won't make any difference. It's too good a story. They'll tell it their way. They'll tell it gorgeous. But if they can't find you, there's part of it they won't be able to tell, and since you didn't kill him, there's no sense your going through that part of it—if we can help it."

"But how—?"

"I'm thinking about it. Don't push me. I've got to figure out somebody to throw them in place of you. So far, I don't have any likely candidates, except Crooked Nose and his pals. I don't know where to find them."

"Who are they?"

"They shot Alex."

She had begun to think sensibly again. "What if you can't find anybody—in place of—me?"

I shrugged, went over and got another shot of brandy. "I give myself thirty-six hours. If I can't figure it by then, I'll turn you in and keep looking for evidence. There's got to be some. If there isn't—maybe justifiable homicide—unwritten law—some damn thing. Got a lawyer?"

She thought about it. "There's Sanders. He was my father's lawyer. I've known him all my life."

Sanders was corporation law.

"No good. He'd turn you over to the cops, find some stuffy, irreproachable character who's handled a couple of petty crime cases and they'd hang you for sure. I know a guy I can work with. I'll go see him."

28

She held out her glass. I poured some brandy in it. She smiled a little. It was the first time, and it was nice. It made her look like a person instead of a symbol.

"What are you?" she said. "I mean—I know you're a detective—what do they call them—'private eyes'—something. But so far you've been so —sort of anonymous. What could I call you? You're obviously trying to help me. But I don't know you. I don't even remember the name on your card."

"Call me Mac," I said. "I'm just a guy. I go around and get in jams and then try to figure a way out of them. I work hard. I don't make very much money and most people insult me one way or another. I'm thirty-eight years old, a fairly good shot with small arms, slow-thinking but thorough and very dirty in a clinch."

"What calls a man to this kind of life?"

"I don't know what called the others. I was a city cop once. Fifteen years ago. I started out in a uniform patrolling a beat on the west side. Wanted to be a detective. There was a guy named Donovan, sergeant then. He liked me and I liked him. He kept pushing me, helping me through the training you have to have to qualify. He'd take me along with him when I was off duty, when he had a case. He taught me everything he knew at the time, which was plenty. When I'd gone through the mill and had my rating, he got me assigned to his staff. We got along fine. If I did anything good Donovan saw I got the credit."

I stopped. I didn't want to talk about it especially. I was only going on because she seemed to relax, listening.

"What happened?" she said.

"A nightclub got held up. The owner—a guy named Pollard—was shot seventeen times. The joint was cleaned out top to bottom. They used trucks. Took the liquor stock, all the cash—everything. They were collecting a past due account. Pollard owed a big bill on a stock of bootleg hooch. After 1933 he didn't need the stuff. He could get legitimate liquor cheaper. So he tried to welsh on the bill.

"Donovan was on vacation. I got a couple of good breaks and cracked the thing wide open. It was all luck. I fell right into it. When I reported on it, I started getting arguments. All the way up—I had to be wrong.

"I was right of course, and Donovan knew it and tried to push it. But we were on the wrong horse. Whoever killed Pollard had better protection than we had.

"When they fired me—for shooting off my mouth to one of the commissioners—Donovan helped me get this license. Being a cop was all I knew. I've done all right with it so far. Thanks to Donovan."

She didn't say anything for a minute. Then she looked straight at me.

"You think a lot of him, don't you?"

"He's like my own father."

She looked away then. "What if Donovan came looking for me? What would you do?"

I hadn't come to that one yet. "I don't know. This murder isn't Donovan's job. It's county work. But he'll probably get into it... I never held anything out on Donovan that I didn't have a right to hold out. So far he isn't looking for you. If you turn out to be wanted for murder, or a material witness and I try to keep you covered up, and if Donovan suspects it —well, I don't know. I hope it won't happen. It will have to be handled to your best interest—not mine. All the times I can remember, Donovan's best interest turned out to be everybody's."

I yawned. I went to the closet and found the folding cot. I took it out into the office, went back and got a blanket.

"The couch is made up," I said. "Just turn back the cover. I'm going out. If you'll give me a key I'll pick up some things for you at your place."

She was practically unconscious. I had to say it twice. The second time she looked in her purse, found a key and gave it to me.

I started out with the blanket. She came out of the chair then, got hold of my arm and turned me around. Her fingers kept working at the flesh of my arm. She looked at me with those gray eyes.

"Mac?"

"Yeah?"

"Mac—who was it that man—Pollard? the nightclub owner—who was it he owed that money to?"

"You better go to bed."

"Tell me, Mac—who was it?"

"It was Warfield."

After a while she turned and walked back into the bedroom. I heard the door click shut and the lurch of the springs on the studio couch as she got into it.

CHAPTER 4

It was three-thirty. The street was dark and the fog floated around in gray sheets under the street lights. I started the car, pulled away from the curb, then slowed and cut the motor until I could hear over it. Somewhere around the corner past Jerry's place another motor started, roared dully, idled. I went on to the Boulevard, stopped, crossed it and halfway down the next block I glanced into the mirror. A pair of dimmed headlights glowed behind me.

I twisted and turned among the streets, using alleys freely and, when I finally got onto a long straight stretch and looked again, I couldn't see anything behind me for half a dozen blocks.

Four blocks away from the Amberley, on a side street, there was a newsstand and an all-night lunch-room. I went in and ordered coffee. After a while a newspaper truck drove up and after the boy had got them out I gave him a nickel, took one into the joint and ordered more coffee.

There was nothing about Warfield.

So they probably hadn't found him yet. Because Warfield would certainly be front-page news. But just to be sure I went on through the paper, item by item. Once in a while they play it sly, try not to break it until they've spread a few nets—especially if they're looking for a hot witness. Donovan would do that.

On page two there was a story on Alex's shooting, not much to it. Donovan didn't give out much until he had his finger on it. It wound up with a story about how Warfield couldn't be reached to notify him of his butler's death.

There was a brief biography of Alex. A promising heavyweight twenty years before, he had fallen into bad company. After losing his punch, he went to work for this and that moonshine outfit, went to jail thirty days—next time sixty—six months—and on and on. Earlier he'd married a little Italian girl.

My mind went back of its own free will, picked it up out of memory. A pretty little black-haired wench. It had filled the papers. Alex was on the way to the top. The girl was a daughter of a poor but honest saloon keeper. Cinderella. Alex lifted her to glory.

He never could fight I remembered. He had long arms and all that bulk that was tough to push over. But he was all tied up in surplus muscle and he moved like an elephant. He'd worked his way up by holding them off till they were pooped and then dropping them with a round-house. When they tried to match him with the champ, Rickard just laughed. And Alex began to skid. On the way down he lost Cinderella. She'd met some of the glamour boys and they liked her. She could sing and dance a little and she went to work in one of the swank spots on the edge of town. One of Warfield's chain. There were some unpretty rumors about that…

I played around with it a little.

He'd had the opportunity. The house evidently got deserted after ten o'clock. He'd had the strength. Maybe he'd had the motive. Maybe he'd had everything. It would be a nice solution because once you'd proved it, everything was all over. No expense for a trial.

But when I got in the car and put away the paper it didn't look so good. He was probably quite stupid. But surely not stupid enough to pay me a visit right afterward. Or maybe that wasn't stupid. Maybe that was smart and I was stupid.

I didn't know. But after that first exciting idea, Alex began to look less and less like my boy. It's hard work to concentrate on a dead man. You keep wanting to forget it.

Life was beginning as I went into Sheridan Road. The street was full of milk and laundry trucks and a brewery wagon with one of those spanking teams that still turn up once in a while almost took my left front fender.

Opposite the Amberley a double-deck bus came up behind me and raised hell when I slowed down. I pulled over to the curb and stopped. There weren't any cars hanging around and nobody was pacing the floor in the foyer. I went on to a side street, parked and walked back to the building. Whistling a merry tune that wouldn't have fooled a Mongolian idiot, I opened the foyer door, nodded pleasantly to a man who was stepping out of the elevator and slipped into it behind him before the door swung to. He would not remember me any more than he wanted me to remember him.

I met nobody in the silent hall on the sixth floor and at the door of 617 I listened for a full minute before using the key.

It was all wasted time. The apartment was as empty as an unrented tomb and just as cold. I went through the rooms fast, to check on whether any of the boys had been around. It was an extensive layout. Fancy kitchen and dinette, full dining room. Living room with big windows— where we'd sat around earlier in the morning. Then a bedroom, ample, and a bath with a dressing room.

Her atmosphere was all over the bedroom. It was nice atmosphere.

I went through the dressing room and bath and there was another bedroom smaller, containing a single bed. It had some atmosphere, too. But nothing to do with her. It wasn't clear cut. There was nothing you could see. Something indefinable, elusive, like the lingering, almost-but-not-quite-gone odor of cigar smoke.

It was a bare room. The bed was against one wall and in the opposite wall was the door to a closet. Beside it stood an old-fashioned chiffonier, somewhat marred and scuffed. A gray throw rug lay on the floor. There was a plain dark brown spread over the bed. I pulled it back. There were no sheets. A folded army blanket covered the mattress and there was a muslin dust cover on the pillow. There was no smell of cigar smoke.

I felt a little better. Still, I had got the impression—it wasn't actually the smell of a cigar. That was only a way of thinking of it. But something —I opened the closet.

Bare as the room, with luggage stacked against its back wall. No odor of cigar smoke.

I selected one of the bags, saddle leather type, less female than the others, dragged it out and blew dust off it, started back into her bedroom. The throw rug slipped an inch. Which was nothing. Also it made a faint, dry rustling sound. Which was everything.

I kicked back the corner of the rug, stooped and picked up the scrap of red and white paper. An inch of it, half an inch wide. Part of a word was printed on it: "...FECTO."

A definite odor of cigar smoke.

I put it in my pocket, carried the bag into her room and began pulling out dresser drawers.

There was a lot of stuff. Some pink, some white, some black. I picked a few items here and there. If I couldn't figure out how the human frame could fit it, I didn't bother with it. I threw the stuff into the bag. When I thought I had enough I closed the drawers and went to a closet across the room. There were forty or fifty dresses hanging there, shoes in a ruffled bag on the door and more shoes in a neat line on the floor under the dresses. Those on the floor looked more practical.

I took down three or four dresses, folded them once and put them in the bag. I reached down for a couple of pairs of the practical shoes and something rustled again.

A sloppy roll of newspaper, braced against the shoes, stirred, wobbled around and flapped open toward me.

I pushed the shoes out of the way and pulled the newspaper across the floor. It was heavy. There were three or four thicknesses and only a couple of them had rolled open. I pulled back the two that were still folded over.

Nestled there among last Tuesday's market quotations was a fireplace poker with a lion's head and throat for handle. The handle end was brassy, brightly polished. But down around the business end it wasn't so nice. It had recently been used for more than stirring up a brisk fire.

I looked over my shoulder at the window. I wanted to sit there and think about it but I didn't want any help and I was likely to get help any minute if I didn't move around.

I dropped the shoes into the bag. I folded the paper around the poker and laid it on top. Then I snapped the bag shut, left the closet and went back to the living room.

The open package containing the book still lay on the coffee table. I opened it and riffled through some pages. There were two columns of type on each page, in an old script. The words were Latin, as nearly as I could make out. The ink was good and black and the paper was in fine condition. Every once in a while there would be a page with some fancy decoration in the margins and along the bottom. What they called illumination, I guessed.

I turned to a page and suddenly felt dizzy. Something was wrong with the type. The top half was all right, but the bottom half looked far away, as if it were in a shadow box—as if the page were an inch thick and had been hollowed out and printed deep inside. I flipped the page up and as it turned, the type that should have been on the bottom disappeared. I bent over and looked and saw a part of the davenport through the page. A piece of it about four inches square had been cut out neatly and with precision. Maybe with a razor.

I flipped another page, another, a lot of them. There was a hollowed-out center in the book four by four inches and nearly an inch thick. The edges of the hole in each page registered exactly with those on each following page.

It seemed like a hell of a way to treat a valuable book.

I rewrapped it, opened the bag and put the book into it, and snapped it shut again.

Gray light came through the half-open slats of the Venetian blinds and fell across the rug. When I opened the door the light fell into the corridor and bounced back off the light walls. It lighted up the thick broadloom carpet near the door and the two little dark clumps on it that were as out of place as the torn cigar band from the spare bedroom.

I knelt and touched them with my fingers. They were crumbly, but still damp.

I had not stepped in any mud myself for several days. Cynthia Warfield was not the type of lady who would have mud on her shoes.

Was she?

I stepped into the hall and closed the door without touching the knob. The bag felt heavy, dragged at my shoulder as I went to the elevator, buzzed, waited, stepped in and rode downstairs. There was nobody in the foyer.

I went up the street to my car and put the bag on the floor. I made a U-turn and got back onto Sheridan Road headed south.

I felt lousy.

So the stuff about the birds and bees was just a lot of crap. And no doubt all the rest of it was a lot of crap, too.

But where had the mud come from? And the cigar smoke? And where had my objectivity gone? My greatest professional asset. Where was that now?

A lot of crap, too.

Anyway, it would either be over in a hurry, or it would be tougher than even I had figured. And I always figure them to be impossible.

I idled past the Amberley, glancing up at the sixth-floor windows as I went by. They were dark. Naturally. But in my mind there was a sort of green glow around them, as around the slits of a cat's eye.

A taxi stood at the curb a block beyond the Amberley. I passed it, speeding up a little to make a light three blocks ahead. A starter labored behind me. I glanced in the mirror and the cab was trying to make the light too. I made it but he didn't, and because traffic cops have very little to do in the early morning hours and therefore don't miss much of anything that happens, he didn't run on through.

While he waited I turned right, into a narrow side street. It turned out to be two blocks long. There was an alley midway along the second block and I turned left into it, went a block, turned again and got back to Sheridan Road.

The cabbie knew the neighborhood. He was waiting for me at the corner. I waved at him.

I crossed Sheridan and went on along the side street toward the lake. It was a dark, quiet street lined with trees. I pushed ahead, going a little faster all the time, till we were hitting a pretty good clip. The cab was a block behind.

Just ahead there was another alley. I braked, released them, turned in and stopped. I counted to three and backed into the middle of the street, crosswise.

The cab's tires screamed, as he tried to stop, couldn't, and swerved crazily, parking his front wheels on somebody's nice green lawn. I heard him swear quietly and at length.

I stepped out, yanked open the rear door and talked toward the red glow of a cigarette.

"Did you want to see me?"

After a moment a man's voice said, "Well—yes."

It was a voice with no poop left. It was undecided, desperate, scared and a plain bluff. I don't know how you can tell, but you can after you've heard them a few times.

"Then pay the cabbie and get in my car," I said. "We won't get anywhere playing tag at five o'clock in the morning." The cabbie had his hand on my arm. I shook it off and growled at him.

"Listen—" he said.

"Yeah?"

"You damn near wrecked me."

The cigarette came out of the back seat. It bobbed around on a level with my collar bone while he pulled out some money.

"How much?" he said.

The cabbie dived at his meter, ripped off the tally and handed it over.

"Five-eighty," he said.

The little man handed him six dollars, walked around behind my coupe and climbed in. The cabbie was still glaring.

"I ought to break your arm," he said.

I held my arm out. "All right," I said.

He looked at it, looked at me, swore some more and went back to his cab.

I climbed in under the wheel, started up and straightened away toward the main streets again. The guy had a fresh cigarette going and he was hunched down on his side of the car, his feet propped up on her suitcase, staring out the window.

"Bag in your way?" I asked.

"No," he said. "No, it's all right."

He didn't say any more until I asked, "Can I drop you anywhere?"

He was having a hard time with it. When he finally made it, you could tell he'd given up on the answer in advance.

"Would you take me to Cynthia Warfield?"

I pulled over to the curb, stopped, turned on the ceiling light and looked him over.

I have seen a lot of them on the ragged edge: shot full of drink that won't intoxicate, or dope that won't take hold any more; guys whom somebody—usually a woman—drained the guts out of and left lying; who had it all given to them until it ran out and when they had to make it alone found they'd learned how. But never have I seen a guy so close to the edge as this one.

Besides being short he was skinny. He was all skinny, including the sandy hair on his head and the straggly little mustache. There was something in his eyes that said he had intelligence, and something right alongside it that showed he'd lost the power to use it for much. He had a funny tic that started around the left corner of his mouth and spread down and out to his scrawny neck. It was irregular but frequent. His clothes were an expensive type but old and half gone to seed. His thin hands shook when he pulled the cigarette out of his mouth or lit a new one.

Altogether he was a man in a blind alley. I didn't know whether my car was the end of it or only a station along the way.

"I wouldn't take you to Cynthia Warfield," I said, "even if I knew where she is."

"You must know," he said. But it was a plea, not a statement. He didn't wait for an answer. "She's my last chance," he said.

"I wouldn't want to seem ruthless," I said, "but it looks to me as if your last chance went by some time ago."

A tight little smile thinned his lips. "The brass ring, eh?" he said. "I think there's one more turn—maybe I can grab it the next time. It's going around very slowly now."

I started the car. I didn't want the dawn patrol dropping in on us with that bag in the car.

"Would you take her a message?" he said.

"Take who a message?"

"Cynthia Warfield. This is her bag, isn't it?" He looked down at his feet.

The initials C.W. were stamped in gold on the top of the suitcase.

"You go right on talking," I said. "I'm beginning to get interested."

"My name is Losche," he said, with a sudden change of tone, stronger, as if he'd decided to make a clean breast of things, as if he still had an identity that mattered. "Herman Losche. I've known Cynthia Warfield for a long time. We were friends once. I was her professor of English in an Eastern school.

"After she married Warfield I began to slip. I slipped very fast and far, so far that now I can never hope to reestablish myself professionally. I traded all that for a life in a world that was completely alien to me—a world of drink, dice, cards and turning wheels.

"Sorry to be so melodramatic about it. For a man like me—born to another kind of searching—it is melodramatic. At first I had the idea that if I could get into a world like Warfield, I could get at him, trick him some way and get Cynthia away from him. I thought, I have a higher native intelligence than most of the people in that world. All I need is to learn the mechanics, the language.

"After five years I admitted to myself I had only the slightest talent for that life. Intelligence wasn't enough; the mechanics and language were easy to pick up, but they had to be combined with a sort of ruthlessness I couldn't command. And on top of all that it was necessary to have a substantial and long-term run of luck. I learned how to cheat in a most masterful way. I can do anything with a pack of cards. But I was neither ruthless enough to cheat the suckers, nor brave enough to cheat the experts."

He lit a new cigarette from the butt of the old one.

"I haven't had any luck now for a long time and, although at this stage I could gladly cheat any sucker who happened along, I lack the capital to undertake it.

"There's a man called 'Burnett'—"

"How much is he into you for?"

"Twenty-five thousand dollars."

After a while I said, "That's a very sad story, Mr. Losche, but so far it doesn't have any point—for me. Did you think maybe this Cynthia Warfield would put up the twenty-five grand?"

"She has done it before—not in quite such an amount. But I don't expect her to give me twenty-five thousand dollars for nothing. I have a proposition."

"Ah. Now we get to the point."

"Now we get to the point…Cynthia Warfield owns a rare book. It's extremely rare and worth a wide price indeed. I know someone who will buy it—for fifty thousand dollars. This prospective buyer is not just greedy for rare items. He wants to buy it to present to a well-known scholarly library, a charity of his.

"I propose to act as Cynthia's agent in disposing of the book."

"I see. For fifty percent."

"For fifty percent."

"Anything to prevent her selling it direct, for no percent?"

"Only these two facts—she doesn't know who the buyer is and the buyer doesn't know she has the book."

"Friendship," I said.

"I am in rather desperate need of twenty-five thousand dollars. Friendship is a luxury to a man in my condition."

"Friendship with this Cynthia Warfield seems to be quite a luxury at that."

"You persist in referring to her as 'this Cynthia Warfield.' Do you really not know where she is? I thought you must know her. You went to her apartment and you came out with a suitcase that I recognize as hers."

I stopped the car in a hurry. I gathered up some of his coat front and twisted him around to face me.

"Look," I said. "That won't do any good. I haven't got twenty-five thousand dollars. Don't try putting a squeeze on me. It makes me nervous and resentful and I sometimes go out of my head."

I don't know whether he was cool or whether he was just so beaten down he didn't care. But he just looked at me and when I released him he sank down against the seat and went on staring through the windshield.

I started up again and we came to Chicago Avenue.

"If you wouldn't mind—" he said, "drop me at the El station."

It was out of my way but I had one more thing to say, so I turned west and drove to Wells Street.

"I don't like to see a guy get the screws put to him on account of money. If—I say if—I ever happen to run into this Cynthia Warfield I will tell her you want to sell her book. Where can she get in touch with you?"

He gave me an address on the South Side, mumbling it. Then he felt for a pencil.

"Want to write it down?"

"I'll remember it," I said.

He opened the door. He wasn't talking to me any more, but as he climbed out he was saying, "Soon. It will have to be soon now. Very soon…"

I watched him cross the walk, push through the swinging gate and start up the steps to the El platform. He went slowly, a step at a time, gripping the handrail, looking up as he climbed.

I swung around and headed back toward the Boulevard. At State Street I stopped for a light and an urchin ran up with an extra—an eight-page spread folded around the late morning edition. I spread it out on the seat and read it in snatches.

"Warfield Dead in Bludgeon Murder."

Half-page picture of Warfield. Short story of the murder starting in twelve-point type and working down to six when they ran out of details. Page two—picture of Warfield mansion. Quarter-page picture of Cynthia Warfield (an old one) and under it: "Have you seen this woman?"

Something very peculiar here. It had taken a little time to get this extra out. The body had been discovered at 4:00 a.m. when a suspicious cop went to the Warfield place after trying for four hours to reach him to no-tify him of the death of his butler. It was now six o'clock and I had only left her apartment around five-fifteen.

What in hell had they been doing between four and five? Shooting marbles?

I read a little farther. One of the Warfield maids had told them Mrs. Warfield had left two weeks before. She didn't know where Mrs. Warfield was living. Neither did any of the other servants.

Simple. Neither did the cops know where she was living yet. Meaning yet.

I went faster, remembered my promise to get her some food, stopped at a place on Chicago Avenue and picked up some sweet rolls and dough- nuts. Then I went about the business of getting them back to her, taking a route down Chicago Avenue across the Boulevard and on to an alley half a block away. I turned on to my own side of the street and parked squarely in front of my business and home address.

On the third of my front steps sat the squat dumpy figure of Donovan. He was resting his big feet on a lower step and his big round head against the iron railing alongside. He might have been sleeping, except that he never does that in public.

I picked up my extra, got out on my side of the car, walked around it and went to sit beside him on the steps.

CHAPTER 5

There was a long period of silence during which I glanced through the paper and Donovan continued to rest his head. Then I put the paper down and Donovan straightened up, smoothed out his hat and stared across the street.

"How do you like that?" he said, grumpy and disgusted. "Somebody finally killed the son of a bitch."

"Yeah."

"I kind of resent it. A day was going to come when I could have brought him in myself. I was going to enjoy it."

"No, Donovan. The day was never going to come."

"Well—maybe. But it was a nice thought, sort of a silver lining. You could look at it in your mind and say, 'What a day!'"

I didn't say anything. I'd had the dream myself. I knew how it felt. Someday you were going to nail all the dirty guys and only nice people would be left. Then there wouldn't be any need for cops and you could retire and live on a farm and get a good night's sleep. Every night. While you still had the strength to enjoy it.

Donovan sighed. "What time was it you went out there?"

"Seven-forty."

"Arrived?"

"Eight-forty."

"Leave?"

"Nine o'clock."

"Alex there?"

"Yeah."

"Anybody else?"

"No. I mean yes."

He sighed again. "Want to start over?"

"No. I forgot—this Mayfair kid was there."

"His broad?"

"Right."

"You talk to her?"

"I gave her a lift over to the Drive. She got in a taxi and went to the Mobile Club, where she works."

"You followed the cab?"

"She got in the cab and told the driver to go to the Mobile Club."

"What kind of a broad is she?"

"The expensive kind."

Donovan looked gloomy. "What did Warfield want you to do?"

I didn't answer.

"All right, skip it… He was all right when you saw him? Felt all right? Wasn't worried?"

"A guy like that—what would he worry about?"

"Me," Donovan said.

"Especially not you. He threw a knife at me."

"What?"

"He threw a knife at me."

"Big knife?"

"Medium size."

"What did you throw at him?"

"Same knife."

Donovan leaned back on his elbows and stretched his feet out to the sidewalk.

"Of course, it was a public service," he said, "so you'll probably get off light. Only why did you smash his face in?"

"I don't want to play any more," I said.

Donovan got up, brushed off his pants. "O.K." He looked at me out of the corner of his eye. "Did you really toss a shiv at him?"

"Yeah, but it was a bad shot. I hit that lovely walnut cigar box on his desk."

"What cigar box?"

"There was one—Big fancy one, on legs."

Donovan looked at his watch. "I been up all night. How about making me some hot coffee?"

"I'm all out. Come over to Jerry's and I'll buy it."

Halfway across the street he said, "Funny thing. I thought you were home at first. Thought I smelled coffee in the hall. Nose must be playing tricks on me."

We went into Jerry's and sat down in a booth. A girl brought coffee whether we wanted it or not. Donovan stirred his for five minutes.

"This guy with the crooked nose," he said, "is called Burnett. He don't do anything much for a living. Gambles some. One thing and another. He's all alibi'd up for the time Alex got shot in the stomach. If we crack that one he's sure got one for the Warfield job, which was goin' on about the same time. So I guess he ain't our boy."

"How can he have an alibi for the Alex killing? I saw it."

"You're the only one, Mac. There's three or four other boys say he wasn't anywhere around here at the time. Me, I think those others are telling fibs. But we got to have more than the word of a shamus to get a grip on him."

He drank some of the coffee, slurping it up noisily. "Trouble is—" he said, "with Warfield, two million people had a motive. Time we get around to all them we will have forgot what we wanted to find out."

He finished his coffee.

"So we got to narrow it down."

"How?"

He gave me a look. "I got a couple ideas… You going to pay for this coffee?"

I followed him to the door. We went outside and stood in front of the place. The light was really daylight by now. There wouldn't be any sun. But we could see by it.

"Main thing right now—" Donovan said, "I wish we could find that Mrs. Warfield. Suppose I'll have to charge her to bring her in?"

I looked over his head.

"I don't know," I said. "Maybe that wouldn't do it. If she's innocent, she's better off not to come in for a while yet."

"Mn," he said and you wouldn't know whether he was agreeing or not.

He stood there a little while, looking more and more hopeless all the time and then he said, "Well, so-long, shamus."

"So-long, copper," I said.

I watched him walk away toward the Boulevard with that short, stumpy, thoroughly deadly stride until he disappeared around the corner.

I started across the street. Fifty yards down, walking fast toward the lake, went a little man carrying a suitcase. I sprinted, using the grass plots along the parking to deaden my footsteps. As he turned into the alley, headed for Chicago Avenue, I was twenty feet behind him.

"Stop!" I said.

He stopped. He stood dead still and waited for me to catch up with him. I walked around in front of him.

He was a head shorter than I. He had a wide, round face, wrinkled and brown, with high cheekbones. He might have been fifty, or seventy. He stood mute, watching me. I reached for the suitcase and a knife flashed in his other hand. I got the wrist, twisted till the knife dropped and pushed him around to face the other way. I took the suitcase away from him and with my fingers against the bone of his arm led him back out of the alley and down the street to the car. I dropped the bag, opened the car door and sat him on the seat, facing out with his feet on the running board.

"Who sent you?" I asked.

43

He shook his head.

"Burnett?"

He shook his head again.

I put my finger along the side of his neck and pressed my thumb in under his jaw. He sat very still.

"I don't have much time," I said. "Let's not waste any of it. Who was the guy told you to pick up this suitcase?"

He didn't say anything. But after a moment he opened his mouth.

There wasn't any tongue in it.

I let go of his neck, pulled him out of the car.

"Run along," I said, giving him a push.

He walked off toward the alley, not too fast, not too slowly. I watched him out of sight around the corner. Then I reached into the car, got the sack of rolls and doughnuts, picked up the suitcase and with the extra edition under my arm, went inside.

There was nothing wrong with Donovan's nose. The smell of coffee was all over the place.

I knocked on the inner door and after a moment she said, "Yes?"

"It's me," I said and she opened it and I went in.

She smiled. She was dressed, except that her hair was down and she was barefoot. That brought the top of her head in line with my chin. She was nice all right. Nice all over. Any other time I would have quit thinking about everything but her.

"Coffee?" she said and I shook my head.

"Just had some."

"Have another."

"Not now."

I handed her the sack of rolls and put the bag on the couch. On top of the bag I spread out the extra edition.

She knew something was wrong but she didn't know what. She looked into the sack, carried it to the kitchen, came back and picked up the paper gingerly. She turned away to look it over. She opened to the second page. I saw her shoulders hunch and draw forward. She folded the paper, laid it on the couch.

"Next step," I said. "Open the bag."

She looked at me, a little startled, then leaned over and snapped open the bag. She pushed up the cover, stood there for a moment looking at the roll of newspaper. Then she worked it open—very slowly with her long slender fingers. Her hands floated up to her face, hovered there.

She held on, didn't crack. She was built strong.

Her voice came, low but even. "Where was it?"

"Your closet. Behind the shoes."

She didn't say any more. She walked away from the couch, stood in the doorway of the kitchen with her back to me.

"Who shared the apartment with you?" I asked.

That brought her around fast. Not quite the way I'd expected. She walked to me, straight and even and looked at me with a level, wide look, and all the finishing school, all the fancy expensive training, all the old tradition stood out like a halo around her.

"You can take that back to the gutter," she said. "I don't know what you're trying to get at—whether you're trying to 'soften me up,' as they say, before you turn me in, or whether you just naturally have that kind of mind. But you'll watch your step with me—Mr. Mac. We're not the same kind of people. I'm grateful to you for taking an interest in me and for bringing the clothes. If you'll let me dress in something appropriate, I'll go now."

"You won't go anywhere," I said. "From what I saw, there was evidence a man had hung around the place. I don't care. It's not my business —only we got a murder mixed up in it now. If you didn't bring that poker home—somebody planted it. If you didn't rub out Warfield; somebody else did. I got to know, that's all. Warfield was bound to get murdered. Whoever did it—it's a good thing. But we have a game to play with the cops. If you didn't do it, then we've got to find who did. If you did it, then we've got to play it another way. Either way—I've got to know. I want to hear it from you now. And put it right on the line, honey. Because I just sent Donovan on his way as if I'd never seen you."

She didn't say anything for a while. She stared into my eyes, looking for something, and I stared right back into hers, trying not to let her find it. Then she turned away and sat down on the edge of the studio couch.

"It's funny," she said, talking to herself, not me. "You say it once and they pretend to believe you. They don't really. They always have reservations. Automatically—a woman always lies at first. That's how it goes, isn't it?"

I didn't answer—because she wasn't asking me.

"Then they think it over—find all the evidence that proves you had to be lying—and ask you again. If you say it the same way again it proves you really are stubborn. You really know how to hold out.

"The third time—I can see how you'd finally confess—just to escape the dreary, rotten monotony of it."

"Donovan smelled the coffee," I said.

She got up and wheeled again in that genteel, defiant way.

"All right! Call your good friend Donovan. Tell him where I am. Let him ask the question. Over and over again. Deliver me. Go ahead! I'm

45

your package. You bought the stamps—with Warfield's money—I guess you've got a right to send me over."

She was wonderful.

I put my hands on her shoulders and pushed her back down on the couch.

"All right," I said. "You didn't kill him. You talk too much, but I guess you didn't kill him. So we'll try to find out who did. We and Donovan. Let's have some coffee."

I went to the kitchen, poured coffee and picked up the sack of dough-nuts. I handed her a cup and put the sack on the couch beside her. We sat drinking the coffee, not speaking. She wouldn't look at me.

Not that I could blame her.

She finished the coffee, set the cup on the floor and reached for her shoes and stockings. She put the stockings on as if she were alone. I had the feeling I ought to turn away, but I was damned if I would. She stepped into her shoes, stood and straightened her skirt. She found a comb, ran it through her hair and put it back in her purse. She put on her hat, her coat, put her bag under her arm, dropped the cover on the suitcase I'd brought and locked it. She carried it to the door.

"Going out?" I asked.

"Apparently."

"Where?"

After a moment she said, "I'll think of something."

"That's the trouble," I said. "You'll start thinking. You'll get a lot of help, too. From the newspapers. You'll think about your lovely, carefree girlhood. You'll think how repulsive Warfield was on your wedding night."

She had her hand on the doorknob but she wasn't moving.

"That won't be so bad. You've done enough thinking about that to be used to it. But then the newspapers will start helping you. They'll tell you how repulsive Warfield really was. After a while you'll begin to wish you had killed him, instead of letting somebody else do it. You'll think about how you only gave him new life, gratified him. Helped him along the road to respectability. 'The princess and the pig'—'Beauty and the well-known beast.' 'Cynthia and Scarpone.'"

"Stop!" she said.

She dropped the suitcase and looked at me. Her face was all misery.

"You think I haven't thought about it? And he *was* a pig. He *was*. But that's all he was. All those awful stories they told about him—those lies—I never believed them. All wealthy men have to put up with that. But he was a pig and it's hard to take. Women like me don't kill. We're trained

46

not to. We're trained to put up with pigs. And I was well trained. He was a pig—but I didn't have any grounds for killing him."

"I guess you've thought about it all right," I said. "But I guess you really don't know anything either. Sit down. Let me tell you about Warfield.

"He started out like the rest of them. Petty. He was twenty-two, or twenty-three when he began. A few cases of rum and gin at first, the development of a clientele among operators of the better speaks, the systematic elimination of less rugged competition until he had a fleet of fast cutters ranging the lakes from Indiana Harbor to St. John's. Once he loaded a freighter somewhere up north with a thousand tons of imported Scotch and champagne. It tied up near the river for a month, while he unloaded as he needed the stock. They brought it off in full view of anybody who cared, in cases marked 'Herring,' 'Codfish.'

"He played rough then. One summer night in the middle twenties he rounded up four lieutenants whose loyalty was questionable, took them out in the middle of the lake and cut their heads off. He dumped the rest of them in the lake, packed the heads carefully and sent them to four of his chief competitors. They went out of town the following day.

"There was never any proof that he ran a brothel business, although in 1926 a girl stumbled into the county hospital with a story that she'd run away from a big house he owned in South Chicago. When they got her quieted down and looked her over they found she'd been flayed so thoroughly that between her breasts and her knees there wasn't a square inch of what you could call skin intact and the remaining shreds were just hanging. They patched her up and sent her to a psycho ward. In there she hanged herself with a piece of the sheet.

"When he got rich enough he cut out all that as a personal activity and went in for the more subtle type of corruption. He was methodical about this too. He saw that the only way for a rich man to achieve respectability and long-term safety was to get into a business in which the merchandise was money, not hooch and women. First he bought the big shots. The story ran that for three years in a row every member of the county grand jury was either heavily in debt to him or right on his payroll. Then he picked up a gang of insolvent but smart accountants and put them to work at the Midwest Building and Loan Association, where he owned a block of stock. They screwed things up fine. He went to the board of directors with enough evidence of illegal manipulations to put them all away for life. Most of them sold out on his terms; those that didn't he let get sent up. Then he poured out enough of his own case to make a good show, posing as the friend of the poor investors. He came out with a ninety percent interest and a name for greatness. For the sake of appearances he let the chairman of the board retain ten percent. At a price. The guy had a daughter, ten years old at that time. They arranged it. Ten years later, Warfield would marry her. That fixed everything up. He built a mansion on the lake shore, north, collected art and books and gave nice, well-managed parties. He was a big name in town. A leading light. Everybody who knew him hated his guts. Loved his money. He was fantastic. They never could get him after he bought that building and loan business. He was too honest. He was the A number 1 bastard of the city and he made it stick.

"His real name was Luigi Scarpone."

While I talked she had been sitting on the couch, staring beyond me at some memory. When I got through with it I glanced at her face. It was a mottled color, mostly white, with blue splotches. Suddenly she got up, rushed past me into the bathroom and yanked the door shut behind her.

She was in there quite a while and when she came out she looked a little better. She flopped down on the studio couch and I couldn't see her face for all the coat sleeves it was buried in.

At the door I said. "Forget it now. I'll be in the office. I've got to do some figuring. Maybe I can solve the whole case on paper. It'll be cheaper that way... When it gets dark we'll go out and get some fresh air."

She didn't look up.

I went to my desk, got out paper and pencil and started figuring on it—on the time. I figured it from every possible angle, for all the people I could think of who might have any connection with anything. My time out to Warfield's—one hour. My time back—forty-five minutes—allowing for picking up the Mayfair girl and two or three minutes' conversation with her. (I wondered how long it had taken her to get to the Mobile in that cab, reminded myself to drive it sometime, just for the hell of it.) My time at Jerry's before I came into the office and found Crooked Nose and his pals. The time I spent with them. Half an hour. The time we left and met Alex coming down the street. That was 10:30. There were two hours of talking with cops, including Donovan, before I went to the Amberley Apartments to see Cynthia Warfield.

I didn't know what her time table had been up to 11:30 p.m.—the time she said she'd arrived at Warfield's. If that was true, and if Warfield had been finished off by Crooked Nose Burnett and Co., then she almost certainly would have met them coming out as she was going in. Because they hadn't got away from my place until 10:30. You could drive to Warfield's in forty-five minutes, if you didn't care about speed limits, but you would have to move awfully fast to crack that gate, get up to the house, kill Warfield and get out the gate again between 11:15 and 11:30.

I wondered how Alex had got down here. When we saw him in front of my office, he was walking. He hadn't walked all the way. He hadn't taken

48

a bus—it would have taken two hours at least. Even if Warfield had sent him out right on my heels, he couldn't have made it by 10:30. A cab, maybe—but cabs weren't thick out in that neighborhood.

I got up and stuck my head in the door. Cynthia was lying on her back, staring at the ceiling.

"When Alex went out alone," I said, "did he use a car?"

She blinked at me. "I believe so… Yes. He had one of his own."

"What was it like?"

"It was a green roadster—Ford, I think. Alex didn't take good care of it. It rattled a lot."

I remembered the professor. "Who's Losche?" I asked her.

Her eyes widened. "Herman Losche?"

"That's it."

"Where did you see him?"

"Who is he?"

"He is—he was—my English professor in school. Ten years ago. Something happened to him—something awful—"

"Yeah. You happened to him."

"Is that what he said?… He was in love with me. He followed me here when I left school. I had to marry Warfield and I told him I was doing it because I wanted to, that it wouldn't do any good for him to try to see me. But he wouldn't go away. He stayed here. He taught for a while, but he had begun to drink a lot and he lost his job. He just kept going down. Once in a while I would arrange to see him somewhere. He would threaten to kill himself if I didn't. I tried to help him. I even offered to set up a private school for him, if he'd go back to work. But he wouldn't listen."

"How much money did you give him?"

"I don't remember. Quite a lot over a period of time."

"How did he know about the book?"

"The book?—Oh—I'd told him about it."

"Ever show it to him?"

"No. I don't remember ever taking it out of the house."

"If he never saw it, I wonder how he knew what it was worth?"

"He knew a lot about books. That was his work."

I told her about the deal Losche had told me he could arrange.

"But I don't want to sell the book. I don't need the money."

"No. He does."

"It wouldn't really help him. It's not money that will help him. It's—it's something else."

"It doesn't matter to me. I told him I'd give you the message."

"What will happen if he can't pay the debt?"

49

"I don't know. Different things could happen. But the guy he owes it to is the one that killed Alex."

She turned her head and studied the wall beside the couch. After a while she got up, pulled a checkbook and pen out of her bag and wrote a check. She handed it to me. It was for twenty-five thousand dollars, made out to cash.

"What am I supposed to do with this?"

"I want you to pay Losche's debt."

"That's a lot of dough," I said. "It's not your liability."

"I know. But I can't just abandon him. I can't let him—be killed—or something just over money."

"He'll do it all over again."

"Perhaps. But I can't close the book on him, Mac. I'd never get another night's sleep—"

I looked at the check. "I don't think Mr. Burnett will take this," I said.

"Perhaps if you'd cash it—"

"If you want to give this Losche a bunch of money, that's one thing. But don't hand over your life, too. If I walked into a bank with this check the cops would be over here before the cash register stopped ringing. They wouldn't cash it for me, anyway."

"But I don't have that much cash—not anywhere. Would Mr. Burnett prefer nothing at all?"

"Don't get me wrong. Mr. Burnett wouldn't turn down the money. But ordinarily they don't go for checks—it's too easy to stop payment. And I don't think he'd be interested in endorsing this particular check at this particular time."

"But anyone can endorse it—" I thought for a minute. Sooner or later I had to see Burnett. Either he wouldn't want to see me at all or he wanted very much to see me in the sights of his favorite gun. One way I couldn't get to him. The other way I was a dead duck. But maybe if I had twenty-five thousand bucks for him—

"All right," I said, "I'll try it. Maybe he trusts somebody that much. It's expecting a lot. But maybe he does."

I put the check in my pocket. She'd dropped the suitcase on the floor at the foot of the couch. I opened it, lifted out the poker wrapped in newspaper and the book in its box. I took her clothes out and piled them on a chair. I got a blanket and a couple of sheets out of my closet, folded the sheets into the suitcase and laid the book on top of the sheets.

"Any names, monograms, labels on that stuff?" I asked her, pointing to the clothes.

She thought a moment. "Some of them," she said.

I got a razor blade; went over each piece, removing labels where I found them.

"Let me have your handbag."

She handed it to me. I went through it carefully, taking out everything that had her name or mark on it. Driver's license, bank book, a monogrammed vanity. The bag itself was plain, no monogram.

I put all the stuff in beside the book. I folded the blanket in on top and closed the suitcase.

"That wipes out the name, anyway," I said. "You don't look much like that newspaper photo. Keep your hair down the way it is. If anyone should happen to push in here while I'm gone, you'll have to pretend you're my roommate. Please don't overdo it. Consider my reputation."

She smiled, looked away from me. "I'm sorry I've been difficult, Mac."

"Forget it."

"Isn't there anything I can do to help you?"

"Yes. Figure out who had a reason to cut a big hole out of the middle of that copy of Mr. Gutenberg's Bible."

"A hole?"

"A hole about four inches square cut out of fifty or sixty pages in a row."

"Oh, no!"

"If the book wasn't worth murder in good condition, what makes it so valuable with a hole in it?"

"I can't believe it! Who would do—?"

"I've been wondering, too." I picked up the suitcase and the poker. "I may be gone quite a while. If you get hungry, there's this stuff I brought. Better not cook anything. I've got informal, hungry neighbors. Likely to drop in if they smell food. So-long. You'll be all right if you can take it easy. Make believe you're somebody else."

"I do feel like somebody else."

"Who?"

She laughed. "I don't know. Some lucky girl…"

"All right. That's better."

I went outside carrying the suitcase and poker. I walked toward the lake past the alley. It was empty. I crossed the street, strolled back toward Jerry's place. Two men sat in a green Packard, facing the lake. They didn't belong in the neighborhood. The car had a New York license. The men looked as if they had been cut off the same piece of cloth as Burnett and his pals, Lefty and Al. I went on and turned the corner at Jerry's place, walked down the side street toward the tennis courts on the next corner. There was a car parked at the curb near that corner, facing my office. A man sat behind the wheel, smoking a cigarette. He was alone in the car. He did not glance at me as I passed.

At the corner I crossed the street again, went back toward my office along the brick wall of the old apartment building that had been converted into offices and studios for artists and advertising agencies. In the middle of the wall were three steps leading up to a side door, now used as a fire exit.

I glanced in as I passed. There was a guy standing on the middle step, staring out at the street.

Casing him was like trying to case the Washington Monument in one quick glance from ten feet away. He was six feet six and probably three feet across the shoulders. He wore an expensive tan gabardine suit and beautiful white silk shirt with a long roll collar. His face was swarthy, almost black. Native Mexican, I guessed. Plenty big, but some of them are. He was smoking a long thin cigarette.

I went on to the corner and crossed the street. I went into the office and across to the inner door. I used my key to open it, calling to Mrs. Warfield as I turned it. She was in the chair reading the paper.

I got a gun out of a dresser drawer, checked to see that it was loaded and handed it to her. The question was in her eyes, but she didn't ask it.

"Know how to shoot?" I asked.

"A little."

"Just in case," I said, "anybody comes in without knocking. Shoot. Shoot straight, without pausing to talk it over. You'll have time to get ready, because they'll either have to pick the lock or break the door down, unless you open it for them, which I wouldn't if I were you."

She looked the gun over and then she looked at me.

"You're not just trying to frighten me, Mac, so I'll stay put?"

"No, baby. I have just noticed that the neighborhood is full of strangers and none of them are cops. I hope that when I go out again and drive away, they will be convinced I have what they want."

"What do they want?"

"I'm not sure. But I don't think they are the type of characters who spend a lot of time reading the Bible—in Latin."

As I went out she said, "Mac—be careful, please."

"Never fear," I said. "I'm probably one of the most careful people in this town. I love life… So-long."

CHAPTER 6

I put the suitcase on the seat and the poker on the floor. I drove to the Boulevard, went up to Chicago Avenue, turned back to the alley and coasted along the street toward the office. The green Packard with the two men in it was no longer there. As I turned into the Boulevard, headed for the Loop, I saw it nosing out of the alley behind me.

At Ohio Street I turned off and went to Rush. I went down Rush to the end, turned around and headed back to Ohio. Over my left shoulder I could watch the river traffic. The green Packard slid past Rush Street on Ohio and disappeared. It would turn and wait for me to come back. That was all right.

I waited fifteen minutes. Then, up around Wells Street I saw a raised bridge. The smokestacks of a tug loomed, passed under it and came on. There was one more bridge to go. I kept one eye on the tug, the other on my watch. I heard the bell on the next bridge ring, saw it start to rise. I started up, crawled to Ohio Street, spotted the green Packard half a block away and gunned my motor. I beat two taxis to the turn, raced to the Boulevard and bullied my way into the stream. One taxi waited, blocking the Packard momentarily. The Packard honked and went around. Brakes screamed. The light was red, the bell clanged and the gates were on the way down when I hit the bridge. I went on through. Somebody yelled at me. Looking back I saw the green Packard, nudging the gate, but standing still.

I took Wacker Drive to Clark Street and went out beyond Roosevelt Road to the Crosley Arms—a very fancy name for a highly questionable hostelry, a little place stuck between a garage and a Thompson's cafeteria; six stories high, with one bath each for male and female on each floor.

I took the suitcase into the lobby. The clerk shook his head as I stepped up to the desk.

"Sorry—" I gave him a folded ten-dollar bill. He looked over his board. "There's a single in the rear on the fifth floor—"

"That'll be fine," I said. "I've been driving all night, got to go out, I'd like to get right in there and grab a little rest."

I signed "James Stephens" on the register and followed the clerk into the elevator and up to the fifth floor. I carried the suitcase. The corridor was so dark I couldn't even see the numbers on the doors we passed. There was a window at the end but its shade was drawn.

The clerk went to the last door on the right, stuck the key in the lock and pushed it open. I went in, took the key, locked the door from inside. There was a brass bed, a chest of drawers, a lavatory and an overstuffed chair. In one corner a small closet. The shades were down and I left them down. I was glad I didn't have to live in it.

I opened the suitcase on the bed, took out the book and all the miscellany I'd taken from Cynthia's bag. I opened the book package, put the other things in it and rewrapped it. I felt the mattress—no springs. I pulled the bed away from the wall, lifted the spread on that side and using the knife on the end of my watch chain, cut a fifteen-inch slit in the lower side of the mattress, just above the welting. I dug in with my hand, pushed the padding out of the way and slid the package in as far as I could reach. Then I patted the slit side of the mattress back into shape, dropped the spread and pushed the bed back against the wall.

Diligent search would reveal it, but there wasn't likely to be a diligent search—only a casual, quick money search. The clerk would probably go through the suitcase. He might be amused, but never surprised. It wasn't uncommon, hotel accommodations being as they were, for a man to carry his own sheets and blanket.

I slid the suitcase under the bed, opened the door, locked it from the outside and went down to the lobby. The clerk was alone, reading a paper. I kept my key, went out to the car. There was no sign of the green Packard.

It was after nine now, a dirty gray day, and the early traffic rush was over. I made good time after I got away from the Loop onto the Drive headed north. A boy in blue on a motorcycle picked me up for a while and we drove along at the top of the legal limit until he turned off and I could stretch out a little.

I rode past the Warfield place without slowing down. There was nothing to be seen from the street. The gate was closed. Unless they had cleaned everything up already, which was doubtful, there would be cars up near the house. Just beyond the north wall of the estate and roughly parallel to it ran a private side road that wound upward among trees and bushes toward the bluff overlooking the Lake. The road was out of use. There were cracks in the macadam with grass sprouting in them. A thick layer of unmarked dust lay over the paved part. Faded grandeur of the North Shore. The places were expensive to maintain. If anyone lived at the end of the road, it was probably in two or three out of twenty rooms.

I cut into the road, taking it easy over the cracks. It would be a hell of a spot for a blowout. I wondered whether Donovan was in the Warfield house. Probably not. He would be out working his legs.

A hundred yards up the road the roof of a small house showed above the wall on the Warfield side. That would be the servants' quarters. I drove on, looking for a place to turn around. Seventy feet farther the road ended. Wherever it had once led, it didn't lead there now. There was a sagging wire stretched across it and beyond that a tangle of shrubbery and tall grass.

It took me half a dozen forward and back starts to get the car headed back toward the street. I coasted downhill a little way, as close to the wall as I could get without running off the road onto the soft ground. Fifty feet short of the roof of the servants' house, I stopped and set the emergency brake. I picked up the newspaper with the poker in it from the floor of the car, climbed out and walked along the running board and up onto the fender. That brought my eyes on a level with the lower edge of the wall's top layer of stone.

I reached across the two feet of space between the car and the wall and laid the roll of newspaper on top of the wall. It would have been nice to know what was on the other side but I couldn't see over it and I didn't want to get caught clambering around. I held my breath and gave the roll a healthy push with my finger tips. It scraped and rustled across the top of the wall and as I climbed back in under the wheel I heard it drop into something crackly on the other side. It sounded like bushes. So it hadn't landed on somebody's head or on top of a greenhouse.

I hoped they would find it soon enough to do some good. It had to be found, preferably with fingerprints, but not Cynthia Warfield's fingerprints and not in her apartment or in my car.

I coasted on down the road to the street. A heavy truck rattled by and I started my engine in the wash of its roar, idled into the street and drove slowly past the estate. There was still no sign of activity.

A couple of blocks beyond the Warfield place there was a gas station. I drove in beside one of the pumps and an attendant came out. I told him to fill it up and when he came up front to clean the windshield I said, "Some excitement around here."

"Yeah," he said, and went around to the other side.

"You ever see the old boy?"

He either didn't hear me or pretended not to. When he came back to the window I handed him the money for the gas and asked it again, "You ever see the old boy?"

"Warfield?"

"That's right."

"Once in a while."

He went in to get the change. When he handed it to me I asked, "Ever see Mrs. Warfield?"

I knew the question had been a mistake by the way his eyes went over me. He shrugged.

"I can't rightly remember," he said.

I drove away. Either he was romantic about Cynthia or the cops had got to him and told him to keep his mouth shut. I doubted that he was romantic about Cynthia. So if it was the cops, I had just furnished them with a four-star lead—straight to me.

I drove to a Loop tavern in the shadow of the City Hall, one of the blacker shadows. It had been open for half an hour and Big Fritz, the "one-legged wonder of the West Side" was leaning against the cash register, picking his teeth, waiting for his dingy trade. I sat down at the bar.

"Hi, Mac," he said, without moving either his body or the toothpick.

"How's business?" I asked.

"Good. It's easier to bum two-bits for a drink than to sit on a bench and feed the pigeons."

"Things have changed."

"Yeah. Used to be the other way round. You want a drink?"

"No."

"O.K."

"Where would I find a guy named Burnett?"

Big Fritz looked at the end of his toothpick, saw it was well masticated, reached for another one.

"Man with a scar?"

"That's it."

He stuck the toothpick in his mouth. "If he's hot, you won't find him."

I waited.

"If he ain't hot, you'll find him out around that joint, the Mobile Club."

"He own it?"

"He owns a piece of it."

I hauled my feet up alongside the stool as the boy came with his mop. Neither Fritz nor I said anything until after he'd finished mopping under my feet and gone away. Then I said, "Thanks."

"That's O.K., Mac," Fritz said.

I climbed down and walked away. I drove back across the river, got over onto Rush Street to avoid the traffic. I crossed Chicago Avenue, and slid by the fronts of the Latin Quarter clubs and the old gray stone houses that looked faded and washed out in the gray light.

I turned left into a wide, tree-shaded street lined with those old two-story houses converted into apartments. The exclusiveness and gentility

56

had gone long ago. Taverns turned up every once in a while; small groceries, and shops clustered here and there.

Three blocks along I pulled up in front of one of the shabbier old houses. It was stained and blotched and its steps were cracked. Across the street, between an alley and a liquor store, stood the Mobile Club. A green canopy stretched from its door to the street. A Negro in a white coat was polishing the brass door handles. I got out of the car and crossed the street.

The boy looked at me. "Sorry, boss. All closed up."

"I'm on business."

He shook his head sadly. "Ain't nobody here."

"I want to see Mr. Burnett."

He grew sadder. "Mr. Burnett especially ain't here."

A faint blare of music sounded inside. The boy's eyes rolled away. "That just the band, ree-hearsin', boss."

"I want to see the band leader."

In another two minutes he'd be crying.

"Not durin' a ree-hearsal, boss. You kin wait till he come out."

A face looked through the heavy plate window. It needed a shave. It was a thick face with a wide jaw. The door opened and the face came out. It was set on a wide body. One solid chunk the same width from the shoulders to the ground. The boy retired, rolling his eyes.

"Want to see somebody?" the face asked.

"Not you."

"Who?"

"Burnett."

"Not in."

"I want to see Mr. Burnett about a matter of money."

"That he owes you?"

"That somebody owes him."

"You got it with you?"

I just grinned at him.

"What's your name?"

"Mac."

He gave me a look. "That's anybody's name."

"That's who I am."

"Wait a minute." He went back into the joint.

After a minute I tried the door. It was locked. I stood around and waited. Every once in a while a blast of that music would come. The sun started out and ducked back under again. I looked across the street at the old house. On the second floor there was one of those large studio windows with drapes. As I glanced up one drape was pushed aside and somebody stood in the window looking down into the street. A man about six feet six and maybe three feet across the shoulders. I couldn't see his complexion, but I guessed it would be on the swarthy side.

The wide face reappeared in the club doorway. A stubby finger beckoned. I went to the door, opened it and stepped into the gloomy vestibule.

The wide one was walking away. I followed him past the hat-check stand into the foyer. Across the nightclub on the bandstand I could see the band at work. Some girls in shorts and halters stood around or sat at tables near the dance floor. We skirted the back row of tables, went through a velour-draped doorway into a corridor past dressing rooms. I looked at the doors. On one of them on a little silver plate was the name, "Miss Mayfair." Over the doorknob hung a sign that read, "Do not disturb."

At the end of the corridor was a flight of steps. I followed him up to a landing and another corridor and we went back toward the front of the building. There were double doors every few feet that led into a big room over the nightclub below. In the room were dice, blackjack and roulette tables. At one end there was a small bar. Some of the tables were cloaked in white dust covers.

I followed him all the way to the front of the building to a blank white door leading off to the left. The guy opened it and stood aside. I went in and he closed the door behind me, staying out.

Crooked Nose Burnett sat behind a desk in the middle of the room. It was a bare room with white walls. There was a davenport opposite the desk and behind where Burnett sat, in one corner, was a safe six feet high.

Burnett's smooth face was pale and not expressive of anything in particular.

"Well, well," he said. "The private eye."

"I've got a business proposition," I said.

"How much do you want?"

"For what?"

After a moment he said, "For the package. The one Warfield's boy had."

"Oh, that. I don't have that package any more. I opened it up and saw it was a book. So I took it to the Public Library."

He held on to the poker face all right. It was awfully hard work, but he did it. Only a slight twitch of his lips and a brief, sudden coming to life in his eyes gave him away.

"What's it about a book that's worth a murder?" I asked.

"You come here to make me laugh?" he said.

"No... You're holding some paper signed by a lad named Losche."

"I am?"

"He said so."

"Go ahead."

"I want to buy it."

"All of it?"

"How much is there?"

He looked at his fingernails. "I'm holding fifteen grand," he said.

"Who's holding the rest of it?"

"Miss Mayfair."

"Why?"

He shrugged. "She's bought into the place here. We call it accounts receivable. Assets. She's holding part of the paper. She don't trust much of anybody. How come you want to buy Losche's debts?"

"I've got a grudge against him."

He studied me with those flat eyes. "Uh-huh. You haven't got that kind of dough, either."

"Let's see the paper."

He went to the safe, fussed with the combination and swung the big door open. There were a lot of drawers inside. He pulled one out and shuffled through some papers, selected a sheaf of them and closed the safe. He tossed the papers onto the desk. I picked them up and leafed through them. There were ten I.O.U.'s for fifteen hundred each, made out to Drake Burnett, signed by Herman Losche. Some of them were a year old. I dropped them back on the desk.

"How did you come to extend all this to a chump like that?" I said.

"I felt sorry for him."

"The hell you did."

"And besides—I knew he could always get the dough if he had to."

"What if he couldn't?"

He shrugged, looked over his fingernails again. "I don't know. It's a good thing you came along. Since four o'clock this morning I'm not so sure he could get the dough."

I pulled Cynthia's check out of my pocket and handed it to him. I didn't pick up Losche's paper. That's the way boys lose their hands.

He looked at the check. He laughed softly. He looked at me.

"You're either too dumb or too smart for a shamus," he said. "You thought I'd turn this down. You don't care about Losche's paper." He laughed some more. "I'm going to take this check, pal. With pleasure. I'm even going to give you ten grand in change."

"All right. I'll take the change."

He was getting a hell of a kick out of this. He chortled as he went to the safe and pulled out a drawer stuffed with cash. He took out some bills, counted them and tossed them onto the table. I picked them up. There were ten bills, each worth a thousand dollars.

"I guess you're smart," he said. "I get fifteen and you get ten and the hell with Mayfair and Losche."

I didn't follow the joke. There was a missing link somewhere. I had a hunch it was important. I put the ten grand and Losche's I.O.U.'s in my coat pocket and went to the door. When I turned to say good-by, Crooked Nose had stopped laughing and he had a gun in his hand on top of the desk.

"Just a minute," he said. "I'm not through. We got something to do. You and me."

"All right," I said. "You're too fast for me. What are we going to do?"

"We got to settle about that package."

"Go ahead and talk. It's your office."

"I got nothing to talk about. There's somebody that has."

"Who?"

"A guy."

"Who?"

"A guy named Garcia."

"I'll be in my office," I said.

I reached for the doorknob. There was an explosion and a 32-caliber hole appeared in the white woodwork just above the knob. My fingers tingled.

"Not your office," Crooked Nose said. "And I can shoot straighter than that in a good light."

I couldn't figure out how I would be any good to them dead. But it wasn't a good time to talk it over.

Burnett got up from his desk and came across the room. He stood three feet away from me—just out of reach.

"Open the door," he said.

There was no percentage in that for me. There would be another one on the other side of it. I was very curious about this other "guy" he kept referring to, but I wanted to limit my engagements to one person at a time. I hate getting boxed up by a lot of nasty people.

"Look," I said. "I'm easy to get along with. Maybe you and I could make a better deal just between the two of us, than we could with somebody else messing around in it."

That was right down his alley. His heater didn't waver but neither did his attention. "Go ahead," he said.

"I've got a book. I don't know what it's worth. If you know what it's worth, you've got the advantage. But that's all right. All you really need to know is what it's worth to you to get hold of it."

He was thinking it over. His eyes developed a far-off, greedy look. Plenty greedy but not quite far enough off. I pushed a little.

"Say the total value of all Losche's paper?"

"Twenty-five grand?"

"Right around there."

He didn't laugh. I wondered how much it was really worth. The far-off look deepened.

"Where is it now?" he asked.

I grinned. "That'll cost twenty-five grand," I said.

He grinned a little too. "Maybe you made a deal, Mac," he said, and he was enjoying it so much that for the tenth part of a second he forgot to watch me.

My foot danced off his wrist and the gun flew straight up and fell between us. He was smart enough not to go after it, but for a little while he was confused without it. They always are.

I slid it out of the way and moved around to his right as he brought his left arm up. I hit him twice in the navel before he got into position and then I ducked under his left arm close to his body and kicked the backs of his knees, first one, then the other.

I couldn't hope to get away with this for long because he was getting angry and I knew he would tighten up, so I tried to finish him off by pounding the back of his neck while he was still on his knees.

I only cleared his head for him. He twisted and came up from the floor with all his weight in his right fist. I saw it soon enough to roll but I rolled so fast I lost my balance, jammed into the desk and slid across the top of it and down behind it onto the floor. He came after me fast. I crawled away with his swivel chair between us, and then let him have it full force in the stomach as he lunged. He grunted, fell across it and grabbed at me, all at once. His momentum knocked me down. We rolled over a couple of times, clawing at each other and just as I jerked clear and climbed onto my haunches the office door opened and the room seemed full of guys— none of them friendly.

Two of them, using my arms like skipping ropes, swung me up off the floor and back against the wall. I stood very still against the wall because I thought my back had broken and that if I moved, my spinal column would fold over on itself. The two of them held my arms tight against the wall and Burnett walked up close and studied me. He was breathing a little fast and only partly because he was winded. The rest of it was plain fury.

The first time he hit me I went halfway out and my head sagged forward. Then each time after that my head would snap back against the wall and jar me awake. I wondered how long I could keep that up. I hoped it wouldn't be long. I kept my eyes closed because they were no good to me open. I saw eight or ten of everything, all of them moving in different directions. The back of my head went numb first and finally my jaw didn't feel anything either. I knew I was being hit because I could feel my neck pivoting under it but I couldn't feel the blows.

Then suddenly I wasn't standing up any more. I was sitting on the floor, propped against the wall and Burnett was saying, "Open your eyes, shamus."

I tried but I couldn't. The muscles seemed to work all right but no matter what I did with them I couldn't see anything. Not that I wanted to.

A full glass of very cold water restored part of my vision. It was blurred and the people were all jumbled up. I knew there couldn't be that many of them. I worked hard at it and pretty soon I managed to separate Burnett and hold on to him. My head felt light and much too big and there was a strong wind blowing somewhere. I knew the windows were closed but could hear it roaring.

Burnett had his gun back. He was tossing it back and forth from one hand to the other. It made me dizzy to watch it. In order to stop it I said, "Go ahead. It's your office."

I really thought he would too. But I couldn't make myself care. He kept tossing the gun around, glaring at me.

The door opened and a new guy came in.

"That fat cop Donovan just drove up across the street."

"So what?" Burnett said.

"So he'll be snooping around. You want a corpse found right in your office?"

"I'll kill the bastard."

There was a pause.

"Kill Donovan?" the guy asked quietly.

I counted to six while Burnett thought about it. He must have thought pretty straight because he put the gun away and went to the door. Three men followed him.

"Al," Burnett said, "stay here. I'll finish the shamus when I get rid of the cop."

One of the three turned back into the room. Burnett and the other two went out, closing the door. This Al walked across the room very slowly until he stood over me. He had a big bandage on one finger.

"Well," he said, practically whispering. "We're all alone."

He leaned down and our faces were close together.

"You practically bit my finger off last night," he said.

"If you don't move your face back," I said, "you'll lose your nose, too."

He just laughed in my face. There was garlic on his breath and I turned my head. This, for some reason, infuriated him. He slapped the side of my

62

face. My shoulders slid along the wall. He grabbed my collar and pulled me back up.

The door opened and I sucked in my breath and braced myself against the sound of Burnett's voice and the shock was even greater. It said: "What the hell is all the racket up here?"

It was Marilyn Mayfair's voice. Al straightened and whirled. He whirled fast for a fat man.

"Miss Mayfair!" he said. He was very respectful about it, too.

"Don't you lizards ever do anything quiet?" she yelled. Then she saw me. "Mac!" she said. And to Al: "What's the matter with him?"

Al just shrugged.

"Who beat him up?"

"Burnett," Al said.

"Yeah?" she said. "How many of you held him?"

Al didn't like the way things were going. But she had him in a low, short grip.

"I want to talk to him," Marilyn said. "Alone. In my room. Help him up.

"But Miss Mayfair—"

"Help him up!"

"I can't get up, Miss Mayfair," I said.

I pushed away from the wall and got onto my knees. My head kept getting in the way, as if I were bumping it into things all the time. After a while I twisted around and got my shoulders against the wall and pushed up from my feet. I blinked fast to keep the room squared up and I said, "I feel better sitting down."

"You can sit down in my room," she said.

She took hold of my arm and walked me across to the door. Al just stood there. I braced myself against the door to rest and Al asked, "What'll I tell Burnett?"

"Tell him to go beat up his grandmother," said the Mayfair. "Somebody he can handle."

We went out and along the corridor toward the back stairs.

"That Burnett," Marilyn muttered. "He'd kill the goose that lays the golden egg."

My mind was barely working.

"I laid a golden egg?" I said.

She laughed.

"No, honey," she said. "Not yet. But somebody did. And if you play nice, you and little Marilyn Mayfair will crack it and have ourselves a time."

"Sounds good."

63

"It is good."

The stairs were tough, but we made them and doubled back along the row of dressing rooms down below. She stopped me at her door, pushed it open and led me in. She closed it behind us and I heard a click. There was a studio couch against one wall and I went to it and sat down. Marilyn poured something out of a bottle and handed it to me. It burned and it helped.

"I never had a lady save my life," I said. "What shall I say?"

"Forget it. I keep thinking we ought to be friends."

She'd make a nice friend, all right, in a way. She was built to be friendly. It would probably cost a lot, but if you liked that type—and we all do—it would be worth it, if you had it. I could see how it would be hell if you wanted it and couldn't afford it.

Well—Warfield had been able to afford it.

She was looking me over. She lit a cigarette, puffed it bright red and stared at me through the smoke.

"Funny," she said, talking into the air. "You being out there last night. Just before you came to your car—that was the last time I saw him alive."

She covered her eyes with her hand.

"Is that so?" I said.

"Yes…I was just thinking—the way we talked about him throwing that knife and all. When I think—I had no idea—" She stopped.

"No idea I might have killed him?" I said.

She jumped a little. "I didn't say that."

"You didn't have to say it."

"Do you know who did kill him?"

"Nope. I don't really care very much. Some of the cops do—strictly in line of duty."

We sat there for a while, she smoking her cigarette, me drumming my fingers on the edge of the cot. The music struck up loudly, the bass blaring. She got up, came over to the cot and sat down beside me.

"About that golden egg," she said.

"Yeah?"

"There's something you could do for me."

I looked at her. "For free?"

"You'll be paid—and well, too."

"I'm always on the lookout for new accounts. Could I take the pay out in trade?"

Her eyes glazed. "Don't let's get fresh, Mac. We're not that far along."

"What did you want done, Miss Mayfair?"

"I want the book."

"Same one Burnett wants?"

64

"I don't know. I only know what I want."

"Could I have another drink of that stuff?"

She got it for me. It didn't help quite as much as the first shot. But it kept my head from going away somewhere.

"What's it worth?" I asked. "In money."

"Oh I'd say—fifteen thousand dollars, to me."

I laughed. "Wholesale, eh? What's the mark-up?"

"What do you mean?"

"Look, Miss Mayfair. You did me a favor. I'll level with you. If I have the book—and I don't say I do—I can't turn it over to you. Because the last I heard, it belongs to somebody else."

Her lips were touching my ear. Her arm had slid under mine. She smelled like gardenias.

"Listen, Mac," she said. "Forget the fifteen thousand. Make it thirty right now and God only knows how much more later. You and me and that money—How about it, Mac?"

I passed. "Who's Garcia?" I said.

I felt her freeze up. "I don't understand," she said. "Maybe you've been beaten a little silly."

"Try this one," I said. "Is—or was—this book the property of Warfield?"

She didn't answer.

"If it was," I said, "you'll get it anyway. Why throw away thirty thousand bucks?"

"What do you mean, I'll get it?"

"I heard you stand to inherit from him."

"Me? Inherit?" she said. "Are you nuts? From that dago? He didn't leave me a dime. It all goes to that wife of his. Prissy-pants Cynthia."

"You don't tell me."

"He gave me a piece of this dump, that's all. So I could work my fanny off. That's all he gave me. And what he took—you should see what he took."

"I'd like to."

She slugged me. It was a good healthy swat on the side of my jaw and it got things down to fundamentals. With the money gone, we could talk about what she really wanted.

"Let's quit stalling," she said. "You've got it and I want it. I'll give you thirty thousand for it. Take it or leave it. If you don't want to take it, I'll find a way to get it from you. I know boys who can do it."

"Boys like Burnett?"

"Better than him."

"What makes you think I've got it?"

"I know you've got it. There's no use talking about that. All we have to decide is when do I get it? I can't think of an easier way for a lousy shamus to pick up thirty thousand dollars."

I got up. This record was broken and the needle was about worn out.

"I'll have to think it over," I said. "If I don't get a higher offer, maybe we can get together."

"Think it over fast," she said. "We don't live forever."

"How right you are," I said. "In the meantime, to show you my heart's in the right place, I've got a little something for you."

"A little what?"

"A little ten thousand smackers."

"What do I have to do for it?"

"Surrender a note."

"A note?"

"Herman Losche's note. Burnett told me you were holding that much of it."

"Where's the money?"

I groped around in my pocket and found the bills Burnett had given me. I showed them to her. She didn't reach. She sat still and smoked her cigarette.

"You give me Losche's paper, I give you the money." She didn't move. "Come, come, Miss Mayfair. Nobody hesitates to accept ten thousand dollars in payment of a legal debt. Or even an illegal debt."

She got up, went to a dressing table and opened a drawer. She fished in it and came up with some paper. She threw it to me and I handed her the bills. I counted the I.O.U.'s and put them in alongside the ones I'd bought from Burnett. She wasn't happy about any part of it.

"All right, baby," I said, getting up. "Maybe I'll see you around."

"Don't bother," she said, "unless you bring the book."

I started toward the door to the corridor. She grabbed my shoulder and turned me around.

"Go out the other way," she said. "You might run into Burnett. I don't want you dead—yet."

"Thanks," I said.

The door led into the alley. I stepped out into the day-light, closed my eyes and held my head very still. It throbbed now, but it felt smaller. My jaw ached steadily, without throbbing. If I looked the way I felt I was Humpty-Dumpty.

I started back toward the front of the club to get my car, thought better of it and walked down the alley to the next street. I turned and walked to the Boulevard. There weren't many cabs and after I'd walked as far as Chicago Avenue, I decided to go on walking. I remembered Cynthia and stopped at the drugstore on the corner and got some chicken sandwiches and cake to take out.

My mail had come and I opened the box and took it into the office with me. I carried the sandwiches to the door of the living quarters, found my key and went in.

The room was spick and span, the coffee cups washed and stacked in the kitchen. The cover on the studio couch was neat and unwrinkled. And Cynthia Warfield and all her effects were gone.

Pinned to the couch cover were a couple of pieces of paper. I picked them up. One was a check for two thousand dollars, signed by her. The other was a note that read:

Mac:

I had to leave. You have to believe it was necessary. Please understand—this check is payment for services fully rendered and I neither wish nor expect you to act any further on my behalf.

Thank you for everything.

Cynthia.

CHAPTER 7

There was an interval of quiet during which my mind jammed. I ate half of one of the sandwiches. I made some coffee and it was terrible. The sun kept going under and reappearing. I pulled down the shades and turned on the light so things would look the same all the time.

After a while I turned off the light and lay down on the studio couch. I snapped the radio on, found a station that gave news highlights every fifteen minutes and waited to hear that they had picked her up.

I knew now she hadn't killed Warfield—not just because I wanted to know it but because as I saw the pattern, it had to be someone else. I didn't know who. I didn't think I'd met him yet. But I knew it couldn't be Cynthia. I thought Donovan might know it too, by now. On the other hand —maybe not. It was the sheriff's case anyway and the sheriff didn't have a chance to bring in a big-shot killer every day. A little enthusiasm could color a whole lot of half-baked evidence.

Around two o'clock a report came from the sheriff's office that no new developments had been announced in the case of Warfield's murder; that Mrs. Warfield was known to have been in the vicinity of the house at the time of the murder but had not yet been apprehended; that several persons thought to have been near Warfield on the evening of the crime had been questioned and their names were being withheld.

That helped a lot. That told me everything. Nothing had happened and nobody was talking. So I could wait a while longer. The time would come when I would have to do something besides waiting. But right now I didn't know what it would be.

I wondered where she'd gone. I thought of the characters who'd been hanging around when I left that morning. I thought she would really have shot any body who went after her, which would have left some signs. And certainly she wouldn't have written the note after they'd picked her up. It couldn't have been the cops; they would have announced it. They had no reason not to.

The more reasons I thought up to make myself feel better about it, the worse I felt. And the reasons I felt worse were all personal. I knew it was crazy, but I couldn't help it. I didn't want any harm to come to her, because I wanted to see her happy—happy and on hand.

I fell asleep. That was something else I couldn't help. And it wasn't a pleasant sleep. It was full of Warfield's face in life and in death, and Burnett's. Once in a while Cynthia's face got into it too, but I couldn't enjoy it, because either Warfield or Crooked Nose or Marilyn Mayfair kept weaving about in the background. This dream went on and on for what seemed like hours. I suppose I was asleep only half an hour altogether. And then something new crept into the dream, a sort of black shadow, very thick, very black and awfully close. And I wasn't asleep any more.

The shadow filled the lower half of the doorway between the office and my living room. It completely filled it—from side to side—with Donovan.

He came in and stood beside the couch. His hat was jammed down tight on his head and his face was all serious. "Mac," he said. "I got to bring in Mrs. Warfield."

I looked up, looked away. "I hope you find her," I said.

"I'm not playin', Mac. I got to. She was here this mornin', wasn't she?"

I hesitated over it. "Yeah," I said. "She was here this morning. But she's not here now. That's God's truth, Donovan, and I wish I knew where she is."

Donovan's face wouldn't believe me. It puffed out, blinked, shook itself. And then it settled down to its natural and justifiable reaction—rage.

Donovan sat down in the chair. He took plenty of time and I braced myself against what I knew had to come.

He started out slow and quiet, as always. "Mac," he said, "you lousy godforsaken Scotchman. You lame-brained, half-cocked rookie. You're a disgrace to your profession and a shame to me as trained you. I ought to throw you into a dungeon for life."

Pretty soon he couldn't sit still any longer. He got up, tore off his hat and threw it across the room. He walked up and down, kicking things out of his way.

"I ought to tear up your license and throw it in your face. It was a sad day for me when you showed up with your britches itchin' to be a cop. Why goddam it, you're nothin' but a shyster, a crook, a quack, a stinking badger artist.

"You knew this mornin' I was lookin' for her. I knew she was in here. I says to myself, 'Mac's got somethin'—he'll play it right. He'll turn her in when the time comes.'"

He came back and stood over me.

"Only a few minutes ago I was sayin' to the sheriff himself, personally, 'I got a line on Mrs. Warfield. I'll go bring her in now!'"

"And what happens? You—you lousy, throat-cuttin' shamus—you tell me she's gone! She ain't here now!"

He leaned close to me.

"You know where you're goin', son? Right now? You're goin' with me to the sheriff's office and you're goin' to tell him right in his face that you hid Mrs. Warfield from the cops, tryin' to be a smart boy, and that you let her get away.

"And the sheriff is goin' to put you away in a place where I'll never have to look at you again. Maybe someday I can forget I ever had anything to do with you. What a day that'll be!"

When I didn't answer he got really upset. He reached for the lamp cord and jerked it.

"Look at me in the light once. Let me get one more look at your schemin', betrayin' face!"

In the light he looked at me. A kind of gray curtain slid over him, made a mask of his face. He went across the room, picked up his hat and came back.

"Who's been beatin' on you son?" he said.

"Man called Burnett."

He went back to the chair and sat down again.

"You're worse even than I thought," he said, but he wasn't angry any more. "You let a punk playboy like that push you around—? Why did he do it?"

"He didn't do it alone."

"All right. What was it about?"

"We had a little fuss."

"I saw your car over there. What was the fuss about?"

"Tell me the truth, Donovan. Do you think Cynthia Warfield killed her old man?"

"What's that got to do with it?"

"Everything. If you still think she did it, I can't tell you what Burnett and I were fussing about."

It was a tough one for him to handle. It wasn't quite fair—but then, what is?

"Look, lad," he said. "Somebody killed Scarpone. Personally, I don't care. But I got to bring somebody in for it. So far, we've got evidence enough to bring this Warfield woman in."

"Enough evidence to book her?"

"Enough to book her, son. Right."

"She didn't do it."

Donovan blew out a long, slow breath. "All right, Mac," he said. "Who did?"

"I don't know."

"That's a hell of an answer."

"I'll have a better one later."

The radio was murmuring. I glanced at my watch, turned the volume up and listened. Donovan opened his mouth and I waved at him to shut up. It was a regular newscast.

"...Police late this afternoon redoubled efforts to find Mrs. Warfield, wife of the murdered financier. Apparently related to the Warfield killing was the murder of a man named Herman Losche, discovered stabbed to death in a South Side rooming house half an hour ago. Found on Losche, a mystery man in what has been called the city's swankiest gang killing in many years, was a letter addressed to Cynthia Warfield at an apartment on Sheridan Road. Landlady of the rooming house where Losche was stabbed stated a woman answering Mrs. Warfield's description called on Losche half an hour before his death..."

I was buttoning my coat, reaching for my hat. Donovan stared at the radio, rage returning to his face.

"I'm detailed to the sheriff's office," he said. "I got no time to chase around looking at unknown stiffs. Goddam it, I—"

"Come on," I said. "We've got to get over there."

"What for?"

"I think this may be the answer to your question."

He griped about it, but he had to go and he knew it. "I'll call and get the address," he said, reaching for the phone.

I pushed him through the door. "I know the address."

I followed Donovan outside and into the back seat of his car. He had a plain-clothes sergeant driving for him. I gave Donovan the address—it was out near the University—and he repeated it to the sergeant. We slid into the Boulevard quietly enough, but before we reached the Bridge the guy had the siren screaming.

"You know too much," Donovan said. "Who's this Losche?"

"He's a gambling professor without much sense. He was a friend of Cynthia Warfield's."

"Why would she croak him?"

"She wouldn't."

Donovan sighed deeply. "All right. Line it out for me. Tell me a story. And make it funny, Mac. I'm tired."

"Losche had a gambling debt—twenty-five grand."

"To who?"

"To Burnett. And to Marilyn Mayfair."

"How old was it?"

"Some of it was a year old."

71

"Burnett wouldn't wait a year."

"He would if he knew he could get it eventually."

Donovan held out his hand, palm up and shook it with exasperation. "Give me big pieces. You give me these little pieces and I forget what I started with."

"Don't push me. It's a tricky story."

"No kidding," Donovan said.

We were on the Outer Drive, making sixty-five. A traffic cop came up beside us and looked in, asking with his face whether we wanted a guide. Donovan waved him away.

"Only fall off that bicycle and get himself killed," he muttered.

"So Burnett waited a year and finally croaked him on account of the debt."

"No," I said. "I paid the debt this morning."

Donovan's eyes glistened. "Who gave you the money?"

"Cynthia Warfield."

"And after you paid Burnett he beat on you."

"Well—yes."

"While Mayfair held your arms."

"Don't be insulting. She saved my life."

"And after Mrs. Warfield paid off Losche's bills, she went out there and croaked him."

"Nuts."

"All right, then," he said, "she didn't kill him."

"That's right."

There was no sense in trying to tell him anything now. He was in one of those stubborn moods; everything anybody said he automatically disagreed with. It's a good trait. Some cops get gullible. They believe everybody. So they get mixed up. Donovan disagreed. But he remembered. And when he started to put the puzzle together he wouldn't have it cluttered up with a lot of extraneous stuff.

"What have you got on the Warfield job?" I asked him.

"What's the difference to you? You got it all figured out."

"Sure. I want to see how wrong you are."

"Mrs. Warfield left the old bast—her husband—couple of weeks ago. After a violent quarrel."

"A violent quarrel?"

There was a pause.

"Who wants to talk? You or me?" Donovan said.

"Go ahead."

"A maid told us that. Big fight. Mrs. Warfield moved out, didn't tell anybody where she was going. The Mayfair broad was living in the house

72

at the time. She wasn't home. I figure that wasn't what the quarrel was about. None of the servants saw anything of Mrs. Warfield after that.

"O.K. We checked with Warfield's mouthpiece. He said Warfield left all his dough to his wife, not even a stick of gum to the broad."

"He only bought her a piece of the Mobile Club," I said.

"What kind of a gift is that? So she could work her fanny off."

I stared at him. "Oh, brother," I said. "You sure you got all the lipstick wiped off?"

He glared.

"Go ahead," I said. "This is good."

"But!" he said, "Warfield—who was a mean old goat on top of everything else—*told* Mrs. Warfield that he was leaving everything to the Mayfair. He called her up on the phone to tell her. Same night he was knocked off. One of the servants told us that.

"We checked with Mrs. Warfield's personal maid, who was fired when she left her husband. She said Mrs. Warfield hated his guts and didn't try to hide it. She told us that one night a little before the big fight and walkout, she came into Mrs. Warfield's dressing room and Mrs. Warfield was sitting there saying over and over, 'Someday I'll kill him. Someday I'll kill him.'

"The night of the murder Mrs. Warfield had dinner with a couple of friends—some lawyer and his wife. I forget the name. She sat around with them until ten-thirty. Then she said she had to drive out to Warfield's place to pick up some clothes she'd left there. These people offered to drive her out but she said no, she'd rather go alone.

"At eleven-twenty-five she drove in to this gas station a couple of blocks down the road from the Warfield place and bought some gas."

"Boy's got a sharp memory. Eleven-twenty-five."

"Pretty sharp boy. Then she went on up to the place and turned in. You can see the entrance from the station. At twelve—the kid was just closing up the station—she come tearing out of the place and down the road like a bat out of hell.

"Attendant in the garage at the Amberley Apartments says she come in fast and nervous, hardly said a word to him, yanked a suitcase out of the car and beat it.

"We checked her apartment, found a little dried mud on the rug near the door."

"What does that mean? She killed him, then took a turn around the yard before she beat it?"

He didn't pay any attention.

"The yard was wet. Sprinkling system been running in the evening. We found the bludgeon weapon—a poker—lying in the mud over against the wall near the servants' quarters. She must have run out there to get rid of it. Got mud on her shoes—left some of it on the rug."

"Was there mud on the poker?"

"No. It was wrapped in newspaper."

"Covered with fingerprints?"

"No fingerprints. I figure a combined case of self-defense and outraged womanhood. She went in to say hello. Scarpone started insulting her. She grabbed that knife and let him have it. That probably didn't do for him right away so she ran for the poker and beat his head till he quit wiggling.

"It don't sound nice and ladylike. But I got to bring in somebody for the murder of Warfield and so far she's the only one could have done it. And no matter how you look at it, Mac, she could have done it."

"Why not Alex?"

"Warfield ate dinner at seven o'clock. Servants told us what he ate. We know by looking in his stomach he was alive until at least ten o'clock. You were gone, Alex was on his way to your place, the servants had gone home. Mayfair was at the Mobile Club. She appeared in the first floor show at 9:50 p.m. She went in her dressing room and at 11:30 she did another show.

"Of course there was Burnett. He could have driven out there from your place in forty-five minutes and done the job. But I don't think he did. For one thing, it gets awful quiet in that neighborhood after ten o'clock and this kid in the gas station don't have much to do but notice what goes on. He didn't notice anybody but Mrs. Warfield going in or coming out of that place between 9:30 and 11:30. Alex came out at 9:30 and stopped for some gas. Mrs. Warfield stopped for some gas at 11:25 and then went in. That's all."

"He didn't see anybody else."

"Not a livin' thing."

The sergeant wheeled into Fifty-third Street and I sat on Donovan's lap. He pushed me off.

"I wonder who lined them all up," I said.

"What kind of talk is that?"

"I wonder who paid out all that dough to get all those people to say the right things. 'Someday I'll kill him.' 'Big quarrel.' 'He called her up to tell her.' 'Between 9:30 and 11:30 nobody went in or came out.' Why, Donovan—it's a whole script, rehearsed and timed. I wonder who wrote it."

"You say she's framed."

"Yes, brother."

"By whom?"

"I can't tell you. But I can tell you what the motive was. It wasn't self-defense or outraged womanhood. It was robbery and kind of a piddling little robbery at that. And it wasn't successful because somebody is still looking for the loot."

"Some day," Donovan said, "we must have lunch together so you can tell me what the loot was and who is looking for it."

"The loot is a book. A rare kind of book. And these people are looking for it: Burnett, Marilyn Mayfair and somebody named Garcia. Until some time this morning Herman Losche was looking for it too."

"All right," Donovan said. "Why don't any of these people find it?"

"Because—I'm the only guy right now who knows where it is."

Donovan pulled his hat down over his ears.

"I figured," he said, "the story would have an ending like that. I knew about the book. But I didn't expect you'd come right out and say you knew where it was. Mayfair told me it was hers and you stole it."

I looked at him. The sergeant stopped in front of a run-down, four-story rooming house and we climbed out.

CHAPTER 8

They had just leaned over to pick up the corpse of Herman Losche when Donovan and I walked in. They straightened up and let him lie a while longer.

He looked even skinnier and more moth-eaten dead than he had alive. There was a funny little twist to his lips, as if he'd been trying to figure out which was the bigger sucker, he or his murderer. I guessed it would probably come out even in the end.

He was lying flat on his back beside an imitation walnut bed. There was a dark, ragged stain on the floor beside him, like the outline of a lake on a map.

"He was stabbed in the back," somebody explained.

Donovan, out of habit, started to go through his pockets and a cop stepped up with a little bundle of papers. There were a driver's license, a couple of movie theater ticket stubs, a laundry list, two dollar bills, a couple of pencils, a deck of honest playing cards and a ring containing two keys, which looked as if they might fit doors of houses.

"One of the keys fits the door to his room," the cop said. "The other one don't seem to fit anything around here. There wasn't anything else in the room or his other clothes. A few pencils, some blank paper and some books."

"Any of the books happen to be a Gutenberg Bible?" Donovan asked, and I looked at him again.

"Huh?" the cop said.

"Nothing," Donovan said.

I bent over to look at the soles of Losche's feet. I called Donovan, pointed. "Mud," I said.

Donovan shrugged. "All right. Mud. So what? Town's full of it."

He asked for an envelope, got out a knife. Carefully he scraped the mud off the bottoms of Losche's shoes into the envelope and handed it to somebody.

"Go out to Mrs. Warfield's apartment," he said, "and scrape up all the mud we found on her rug by the door. There ought to be some loose nap or threads in it. Run it over to the lab, along with this here, and see what you can see."

The guy started out. I picked up the ring with the keys and tossed it to him. "See whether one of these will let you into the apartment," I said.

He looked at Donovan.

"Do what the man says." Donovan told him: "He's got a theory. I guess it's all right. He's got a license."

Nobody laughed but me. Donovan looked at me bitterly. He gazed around at the various junior officers and said, "This shamus is a bright boy. I want everybody to watch him carefully, see how he operates. He has got a special technique that ordinary civil service cops can't use. He don't have to think. He just imagines how he'd like things to be and then dreams up a lot of evidence to make it look good."

Everybody laughed but me. Donovan looked at the floor, made a movement with his foot. "Get this stiff out of here," he said. "It's depressin'. I seen too many of 'em in the last eighteen hours."

They got rid of it.

"Where's the landlady?" Donovan asked.

"She's in her own apartment downstairs," somebody said. "She said Mrs. Warfield came up here around 2:30, stayed about ten minutes and left. She left in a hurry."

"What kind of a landlady is that?" Donovan said. "She sees everybody that comes in and goes out?"

Nobody answered.

"How'd she know it was Mrs. Warfield?"

"Said she recognized her from the pictures in the paper."

"Nobody else came up?" I asked.

"Not a soul, she said."

I looked at Donovan.

"We'll go talk to her," Donovan said.

I followed him down three flights of stairs to an apartment at the front of the building. The stairs made a lot of noise. Donovan knocked and a tall, thin woman opened the door. She was dreary looking, a dead pan.

Donovan showed her his badge.

"I already told everything I know," she said.

"I want to hear it again," Donovan said, walking in.

We sat down on a sofa and after a moment the woman closed the door and sat down in a straight chair at a desk.

"You say you saw Mrs. Warfield come in?"

"I did."

"What time?"

"About 2:30."

"Do you look at everybody that comes in?"

"No. I just happened to be sitting by the window and I noticed her because she was so well dressed. You don't see many women dressed like that around here."

"How long did she stay?"

"About ten minutes. When she went out she was in a hurry. I heard her running down the stairs and then the front door slammed and I saw her run down the steps and up the street."

"When did you decide she was Mrs. Warfield?"

"I thought there was something familiar about her when she came in. I looked in the paper and saw this picture of her. Then I knew."

"You knew the police were looking for her?"

"I'd read it in the paper."

"Then if you were sure it was Mrs. Warfield, why didn't you call the police and tell them you'd seen her?"

"I called them as soon as I discovered Mr. Losche."

"But that was quite a lot later, wasn't it?"

"About half an hour, I guess."

"So you had half an hour to think about calling the police to tell them about Mrs. Warfield."

"Well—I—I don't like to get mixed up in somebody else's troubles. And I might have been wrong."

"But you didn't hesitate to tell them you were sure it was Mrs. Warfield who came to see Losche."

"I'd had time to think it over."

There was some silence. Donovan sat scrunched down on the davenport with his ankles crossed. He hadn't taken off his hat and the rear brim was all squashed up flat against the back of his head.

"What was it led you to go up to Losche's room?" I asked. "You visit your tenants every day?"

"Of course not."

"What reason did you have to go up to Losche's room today? After he was dead?"

"I didn't know he was dead."

"Nobody said you did."

"I went up to find out whether it really was Mrs. Warfield. I was—I was just curious."

"What paper was it you saw Mrs. Warfield's picture in?"

"She's been in the papers—"

"I know. You said you saw her come into the house, then you looked in the paper and that's what made you think it was Mrs. Warfield."

"It was this paper."

She pointed to one on the desk. I went over and looked at it. It was the home edition of an evening paper. I looked at the landlady. "Who came in after Mrs. Warfield had gone?" I asked.

She jumped—not much—just enough.

"Nobody," she said. "Not a soul."

"Let's straighten it out," I said. "You saw Mrs. Warfield come into the house. You thought she looked familiar. You looked in the paper and saw a picture of her. Then pretty soon Mrs. Warfield came down and went out. Is that right?"

"Yes."

"You looked in the paper. You saw Mrs. Warfield leave. Half an hour later—that would be about 3:15—you went up to Losche's room and found him dead."

"That's right."

I threw the paper down on the desk. "But this paper doesn't get off the press till 2:30 in the afternoon. It couldn't be delivered to you until three o'clock. Fifteen minutes after Mrs. Warfield was gone."

She flared up. "Well, all right. Maybe it was later. What difference does that make? I can't remember every minute of time."

"Sure," I said. "But you didn't have any doubts about anything till I started asking questions."

"What are you driving at?" she asked.

"Only two things," I said. "Two simple little things. Who came into the house after Mrs. Warfield had gone? And who came in *before* Mrs. Warfield?"

"Nobody, I said."

"I don't believe that."

"Well, it's true!"

"The hell it is. Mrs. Warfield came in, went upstairs, came down and went away. And then—somebody else came in, carrying this paper, gave you the paper and pointed out Mrs. Warfield's picture. Isn't that right?"

"It's ridiculous. I never—"

"How much was it worth?" I asked. "How much did he pay you to remember that the woman who came in looked like the picture of Mrs. Warfield? How much?" She puffed way up, glared at me, then at Donovan, who nodded.

"Go ahead," he said, "answer the question."

She stayed puffed for a few seconds, then she collapsed. "A thousand dollars," she said, whispering so I could barely hear it.

"What did he look like?"

"He was a big man. His shoulders were broad. He needed a shave."

"What did he tell you?"

79

"He brought me the paper—the way you said. He told me he'd seen Mrs. Warfield come in and he hoped I would remember that. I asked him whether he was a policeman and he laughed and said no, he was a reporter. This would be a great scoop for him, he said. Then he laid a bill down on the desk. He said that was so I would remember Mrs. Warfield and forget him. He said it would spoil his scoop if anybody found out he'd been here. After he left I went to the desk and looked at the bill. It was a thousand-dollar bill."

Donovan had uncrossed his ankles, moved forward to the edge of the sofa, and sat with his hands hanging down between his knees. He didn't say anything. The landlady looked at us, ran her finger along a pleat in her skirt and "Do I have to give up the thousand dollars?" she asked.

"Not necessarily," Donovan said. "If you'll come clean with the rest of it."

"But I've told you everything I know—"

"Not quite. Who else came in—before Mrs. Warfield?"

"If anybody did, I don't know," she said. "I wasn't here."

"Where were you?"

"I went to the market," she said, "about one o'clock. I didn't get home till just a few minutes before I saw Mrs. Warfield—around twenty minutes past two."

"They'd remember you at the market?"

"They ought to. I shop there every day."

"The only people you saw were Mrs. Warfield and this guy that came in and slipped you a grand note?"

"That's right."

The landlady followed us to the door. "What if he finds out I told about him?" she asked.

Donovan shrugged. "I don't know. He might want his thousand bucks back. That's a lot of dough for a newspaper reporter."

"Should I give it to him?" she said.

"Well—" Donovan said. "I wouldn't spend it for a couple of days."

The telephone rang. It rang two or three times and finally the landlady answered it. We stood there.

"Is one of you named Donovan?" she asked.

"That's me."

He walked across the room and spoke into the telephone, grunted once or twice and hung up. He came back and opened the door.

"Hang around," Donovan told her. "We'll want to visit with you some more."

We went out into the vestibule. Donovan looked at me out of the corner of his eye, shoved his hands in his pants pockets and stuck out his stomach. "O.K., Mac," he said. "The stuff I scraped off Losche's shoes matches the stuff on the rug at Mrs. Warfield's. That key Losche had opened the door to her apartment. What else have you got figured out?"

"Nothing I can tell you without incriminating myself. The big boy who paid off the landlady works for Burnett. I wish you'd run out and ask that gas-station attendant how much somebody paid him to remember Mrs. Warfield and forget somebody else."

"Yes, sir," Donovan said. "Anything else we can do for you?"

"One more thing. Find Mrs. Warfield."

He looked at me. "Before this Garcia finds her."

I went outside and started looking for a taxi.

CHAPTER 9

The cab took a leisurely route through Jackson Park to the Outer Drive. We coasted into the traffic on the Drive and went along with it, no harum-scarum, no jerking. At Thirty-fifth Street we got into a jam. We inched along, starting and stopping and finally the cabbie decided to get out of it. He turned off the Drive and took Thirty-fifth to the Boulevard.

We stopped for a light and he turned around and said, "I don't know whether you care, but we got a whole caravan following us."

"Maybe it's just that time of day," I said.

"Huh-uh. A guy in a Ford station wagon picked us up at Fifty-fifth and Ellis, just after you got in. There was a green Packard tailing us when we left the park. Now there's a dame in a cab behind us and one lane over. The cab was parked with her in it about a mile back up the Drive. It moved in behind us."

I didn't say anything. I looked back over my shoulder at the cab, but it was the wrong angle. I couldn't see the woman in the back seat.

"Want me to lose 'em?" the driver asked.

"I guess not. They know where I live. That's where I'm going."

"All right, if you say so."

"You know where the Mobile Club is?"

"Sure."

"We'll go by there."

It took us half an hour to get through the rush-hour traffic on the Boulevard and across the Bridge. By then it was nearly dark. I glanced back as we went up over the bridge. There was a cab close behind us. I couldn't tell whether it was the same one. Two stoplights back the green Packard waited for the change. I couldn't see a Ford station wagon.

We left the Boulevard and headed for the Mobile via Rush Street.

"Green Packard still coming," the cabbie said.

He was getting a little nervous. It would be a good idea to get away from him.

He turned left and we coasted past the Mobile. The canopy was dark and no light showed through the door. It wouldn't open till after seven-thirty. My car was parked where I'd left it across the street.

The street was deserted. There were lights in the old houses, but the shades were drawn and only their edges were outlined in dull white or yellow. The street lights hadn't been turned on yet.

We turned around, headed back toward the Boulevard. I paid the cabbie, advised him not to hang around and waited till he was gone. Then I walked back on the sidewalk fifty or sixty feet to my car. I opened the door, glanced at the house that faced the Mobile Club across the street. The drapes were drawn across the big studio window and behind the drapes and around their edges light glowed, as in other houses on the street.

Behind me on the walk I heard the busy click of high heels. I swung into the seat of the car. A girl passed, walking rapidly, her bag swinging at her side. Her steps crackled in the silent street. Somebody's stenographer coming home from a day at the office. She went on and faded out of sight.

I started the car and turned into the alley beside the club. There was a dim red light hanging over the recessed stage door. I passed it slowly. A man stood under the light against the door, a big man, about six feet six and three feet across the shoulders. He wore a tan gabardine suit and a beautiful white silk shirt with a roll collar. The red light splashed over his thick brown face, lighted the cheekbones, made the hollows black. He was smoking a long thin cigarette.

I stopped the car, leaned out the window. "Señor Garcia?" I said.

He didn't answer. I couldn't see what his eyes did, but the rest of his face wasn't paying any more attention than if I hadn't been there at all. He took a long drag on the cigarette and dropped it on the ground at his feet. The door behind him opened and he went through it without turning and then it was closed again and I was alone.

I went on through the alley and turned into the street. I stopped at a newsstand for a late paper and drove on down Chicago Avenue to the alley, through to my own street and up to the office. Parked ahead of me with three cars in between was a Ford station wagon. As I climbed out of the car a taxi rolled past the office, stopped, backed a little and turned into the street opposite my building. It stopped against the curb. I went up the steps to the vestibule. Nosing into the street from the Boulevard came the green Packard.

I went on inside without benefit of lights. I checked the place carefully and found no visitors. I sat down on the studio couch in the dark and drank a shot of brandy. I wanted to turn the radio on to get last-minute news, but I didn't want the noise. I wanted to be able to hear other things.

I checked the gun I had left with Cynthia earlier in the day. I laid it beside me on the studio couch and took another shot of brandy. I got up and went to the kitchen and looked out the back window along the areaway leading to the alley. There were garages on both sides of the areaway with entrances off the alley. Two men strolled out from behind one of the garages past the areaway and on behind the next garage. I waited. Pretty soon they came back across the areaway, strolling in the opposite direction. I went back and sat down on the studio couch.

There was no way to tell whether somebody was going to come in or whether it was all figured just to get on my nerves. They'd had plenty of chances to jump me all afternoon. Of course, sometimes it was better to wait till after dark.

All right. It was after dark now.

The building was about as noisy as a graveyard in the early morning. Most of the other tenants went to work late and didn't come home till nine or ten.

The telephone rang and I grabbed it.

"Hello, Mac?"

"Yeah, Donovan."

"All right. The heat's off Mrs. Warfield. We cracked the lad in the gas station. Same story we got from the landlady. Somebody drove up to Warfield's in a cab about ten-thirty. He didn't see who it was. Fifteen minutes later the cab came back, going fast. Losche tracked some mud around Warfield's study."

"Who paid off the gas-station kid?" I asked.

"Sounds like the same guy. So like I say, the heat's off your client. Let me have the rest of the story."

I told him all of it. He grumbled a lot but he was writing it down. When I finished he said, "See you later, lad. I got to spread a little net."

"For a dead man?"

Donovan laughed.

"Losche had somethin' to do with it. But he wasn't alone. And whoever was with him knocked him off later... So-long, shamus."

"So-long, copper."

I hung up, feeling lonely.

Donovan was happy, which meant he was near the end. He knew who he wanted, but he still had to set a trap. Setting traps was his favorite sport and he was a master.

I wasn't so good at it. It looked now as if I had set my own and were sitting right in the middle of it. I thought it would be smarter to make a break and get out of the place than just to sit there. But I couldn't think of any place to go.

I went into the office and looked out the front window into the street. The green Packard was parked up the street opposite the alley. As I watched the back door of the Packard opened and two men got out. They stood on the sidewalk, stretching their arms.

I went through the living room to the back door and looked out there. The two gentlemen in the alley paced by the areaway, disappeared, came back and stopped. One of them held up his wrist and studied it. He pulled a cigarette lighter out of his pocket, flicked it and studied his wrist in its light. He snapped it dark and the two of them stood there while I counted to three. Then they both turned into the areaway and came very slowly toward the back door.

I went back to the studio couch, picked up the gun and flicked off the safety catch. I started into the kitchen and the telephone rang again. I cursed it and jumped across the room to get it before it could rattle again.

I said, "Hello, I'm busy—" And somebody said, "Mac—oh—Mac!" in a long, tired sigh.

It was her voice.

"Where are you?" I asked.

"Somewhere on Sixty-third Street. Mac—I'm sorry—somebody's been following me all afternoon. I went to Losche's room—"

"I know," I said. "You got a taxi waiting?"

"Yes, but—"

"Go to the Tivoli Theater. Buy a ticket and go in and sit down in the last row downstairs. I'll meet you there. Stay there. No matter how long it is—stay there."

"All right—You will come, Mac? Really?"

"Yes, baby. I'll come.

Somebody tried my back door. It was locked and they didn't try again. I hung up the phone.

At the front door there was a knock, a sharp knock, repeated three times. I went away from the phone, stood in the doorway between the office and living room.

"Come on in," I called.

Somebody was fooling with the lock on the back door. It wasn't much of a lock. It wouldn't take long. I could handle it one entrance at a time but if they came in both front and back it wouldn't be so pleasant.

I slid across the living room to the corner of the wall beside the door into the kitchen. I looked around the wall at the back door. The two of them were standing on the top steps, one of them working on the lock, the other watching him. There was a shadow along one wall of the kitchen. It wasn't much of a shadow. But it would have to do.

I dropped to my knees and crawled into the shadow, my shoulder brushing the wall. It was only eight feet to the door, but it might as well have been a mile. As my knees hit the floor a heavy shoulder battered my front door. I figured three batters would knock it in.

The shadow worked out all right. I crouched in the corner on the knob side of the door. I held the muzzle of my gun about six inches back from the keyhole and squeezed. It was very loud. But as it died away I heard the echoing yell of the one whose hand had been in the way and the clink of a key ring dropped on the stone steps. I hugged my corner and the one they fired through the door splintered and whined its way across the kitchen without touching me.

My blast had destroyed the lock. The door opened outward and I put my foot against it and shoved hard. One of them fell down the steps. I couldn't hear or feel the other one. I followed the door out and they were both off the steps, one standing, the other getting up. I kicked the gun away from the standing one and held my own out so they wouldn't miss it.

"Hold 'em way up, turn around and scram to the alley," I said.

They put their hands up and turned around, but they didn't do any walking. I kicked the one on the left back of the knees and gave him the pistol barrel behind his ear. He crumpled without a sound.

"It's late now," I told the other one, "we've got to run."

I pushed him and he moved. But I had to keep pushing. He was a very reluctant runner.

"Somebody waiting for us in the alley?" I asked. "Call him."

We were ten feet from the alley and he held out for half the distance. Then he stopped suddenly and said, "Lefty!"

Lefty stepped out from behind one of the garages.

"Tell him to drop the gun and stand still," I said.

The guy told him.

Lefty said, "What the hell—" And dropped the gun.

There were voices and pounding feet in my house. I pushed my gun up against Lefty and picked up Lefty's gun. I backed away across the alley into a passage between a theater and store building facing on Chicago Avenue.

I was halfway along the passage before they started coming out of my back door. Then I turned and ran on to Chicago Avenue into the light of the theater marquee. There was a line at the box office and I pushed through it and walked fast to the Boulevard and across it to Walgreen's.

A taxi idled around the corner into the Boulevard and I was inside before it stopped.

"Tivoli Theater," I told the driver. "In fifteen minutes."

He looked back at me sadly.

"If you want to catch those early shows," he said, "you better get started a little sooner."

"You drive it," I said. "I'll do the thinking."

He made pretty good time at that. It was the dinner hour; traffic was light on the Boulevard and when we got onto the Drive we had it practically to ourselves. In a clear stretch I looked back and there were no green Packards or Ford station wagons. It was probably temporary, but it felt good while it lasted.

Anxious to please, the cabbie took Fifty-ninth to Cottage Grove, avoiding Sixty-third, and we passed the Tivoli on the wrong side of the street within half an hour of the time he'd picked me up. He turned around and brought me back under the lights. I paid him across the top of the seat, giving him an extra couple of bucks.

"I won't be in here long," I said. "If you want to drive around the block and park back up the street a ways, you can take me back downtown. There'll be a woman with me. Don't waste any time getting here when you see us come out."

He looked at me naughtily. "Eloping?"

"That's right. Right out of the Tivoli. Eloping."

"O.K., Mac."

I stepped out, made the space between the curb and the box office in four steps and got a ticket. It must have been a lousy picture because there certainly wasn't any crowd.

I stood just inside the doors, beside the back row of seats and pretty soon it got so I could see. There was a man on the aisle in the center section, three vacant seats, then a couple of soldiers, then a boy and girl necking.

I looked around to the left. The aisle seat was vacant. In the second seat there was a woman. She wore dark glasses and her hair hung down around her shoulders. Because dark glasses were a hell of a thing to be wearing at a movie I sat down beside her. For a while we sat there, neither of us moving. I watched the screen, but I couldn't tell what was going on.

A cold hand reached out and lay on one of mine and I got my fingers around it and squeezed. Then her head came over, the glasses dropped off and her face was against my shoulder; her free hand clung to my coat. She was trembling and I put my arm around her shoulders and held her.

"Take it easy," I whispered. "It's all right. What's the picture about?"

I felt her shake her head against my chest. "I don't know," she said.

"That's good. Then you won't miss anything if we leave."

"Do we have to leave, Mac? They'll just be waiting for us outside. It'll start all over again."

"If we don't leave, they'll come in after us—sooner or later."

"But—there's no place to go."

"Yes, there is, baby. And I've got a car to go in."

She straightened up and wiped her face. She groped for the glasses and I took her arm and helped her up.

"Forget it," I said. "Dark glasses at night are as good as a neon sign."

We went through the lobby, paused by the box office and strolled out under the marquee. As we reached the curb the cab glided up and stopped and the back door opened. I helped her in, followed and slammed the door.

"Nice timing," I told the driver. "Now all you have to do is twist around here until you lose whatever is following us and wind up in the vicinity of Twelfth and Clark. Stick to the well-lighted streets."

"Who's following us?" he asked, suspicious.

"Somebody," I said. "You'll notice it."

Cynthia was huddled in the corner of the seat. She didn't have much starch left. God knows what she'd thought about all that time. I didn't press her about it. We rode for a few minutes without talking and after a while she said, "I didn't call you, Mac, just because I was scared. Really."

"Sure," I said. "What made you leave in the first place?"

She studied her hands. "I had a telephone call from Herman."

"Losche?"

She nodded. "Somehow he'd found out who you were and guessed I was there. That was about noon. He sounded awfully desperate—it was horrible. I pitied him so. And that was the most horrible thing of all."

"Did you tell him you'd arranged to pay the debt?"

"Yes."

"And that didn't make him feel any better?"

"No. He said he was afraid it was too late. He knew they were going to kill him."

"He say who 'they' were?"

"No. He said he didn't really care any more, but he had to see me before it—happened. He said he had a confession to make."

"He certainly did."

"What?"

"Later. Go ahead."

"He said he wasn't afraid to die, but he didn't want to die without making this confession."

"Better he should have made it to the cops."

There was a pause. I looked through the back window. Four or five blocks behind us was a pair of headlights. While I watched they turned off. The street was dark beyond them.

"After all, Mac—he'd been my friend. I couldn't ignore him. He sounded so—so beaten."

"He was dead when you got there?"

"Yes, with blood on the floor under him and his feet sticking up—I almost called you, then, Mac. I thought I wasn't going to be able to take any more."

The driver looked around. "I think I lost 'em, Mac."

I looked back. There was a cab not far behind.

"Stop here," I said and he did.

We sat for a few minutes. The cab passed us and went out of sight. Another car drifted up, paused, turned the corner and disappeared. There was nothing else to wait for.

"Good," I said. "Go ahead."

"All the time," Cynthia said, "I was being followed. The cab driver told me. He tried to get rid of them, but he couldn't. Then he got suspicious and pretty soon he recognized me. He said it was his duty to turn me over to the police. I told him all right, if he had to, but I hoped he would call Lieutenant Donovan instead of just leaving me—at a local station. He agreed to do it. We went into a drugstore and while he was talking I slipped away, bought the dark glasses and got another cab."

"You're fast on your feet," I said.

"I was half-crazy. It was like a dream. I didn't understand. If the police were following me—if they knew who I was, why didn't they just pick me up and put an end to it?"

I hesitated over it, but there wasn't much point. "It wasn't the police, baby."

"Then who—?"

"I'm not sure who they are—by name. But they want the book. And back of them all is a man named Garcia."

"The book," she said, whispering. "The book—that's the real reason I called you. I remembered something about the book."

The cab stopped at the corner. I paid him and we walked down the street toward the Crosley Arms Hotel. Cynthia clung tightly to my arm.

"Where are we going?" she asked.

"We're going to get something to eat and then we're going up to my room in that hotel. It's not fancy, but it's out of the way. And it will be a good place for you to tell me about the book."

I held the door of the cafeteria for her and she walked in as if she'd eaten in places like that all her life.

She was some woman.

CHAPTER 10

She ate a good meal. It made me feel better, just watching her. Halfway through it she looked up, did a double take and said, "Mac! You're hurt! I hadn't noticed. That's terrible of me—"

"Not much," I said. "I'm hard to hurt."

"Who did it?"

"Some distant acquaintances. Let's not make anything out of it."

"All right… What were you saying about Herman—confessing?"

I chewed some bread, drank some coffee. "He planted the poker in your apartment. He evidently helped Warfield out of this world."

"No!"

"I'm afraid so."

Her face went gray. When her voice came it whispered huskily. "He was bitter about it—when I married," she said. "But not against me. I thought—I've tried to help him."

"It's all right now," I said. "Donovan knows what happened. Where did Losche get the key?"

It took her a long time. She said it all into the plate in front of her on the porcelain-top table, not to me.

"It's the only thing I lied to you about, Mac. Because I thought it wasn't important—and it was important to me, what you thought about me." She smiled a funny little smile. "In my youth," she said, "that remark would have been considered inexcusably forward."

"Please go on," I said.

"A little while after I moved to the apartment, Herman came to see me. He wasn't—in very good shape. I was afraid to have him wandering around the streets. So I let him spend the night in that extra bedroom.

"The next day I wanted to give him something to eat and I was out of coffee. He offered to go and get some and I gave him the extra keys, one for the main entrance and one for the apartment. When he came back I'd forgotten the keys. It was two or three days before I remembered, but then I didn't worry. I'd never had anything to fear from him. He was embarrassingly solicitous."

"Yeah—even to the point of dropping the murder weapon in your closet."

90

She shivered. "I remembered one thing about that night Herman spent in the apartment. He was smoking cigars. I never liked cigars and I asked him not to. He stopped then, but after I went to bed, I smelled cigar smoke again. I think he sneaked one before he went to bed."

What with the food and seeing her sate, one thing and another, I felt good. I grinned at her, and she smiled back.

"Mac," she said, "that's the first time I've seen you really break into a smile."

I laughed. "I feel pretty good," I said. "All points are cleared up now except one little thing."

"What's that?"

"The hole in the book."

"I don't know why the pages were cut, Mac. But there's something—" She looked around. We were among the last diners and some of the lights had already been turned off.

"Must we sit here? You said you had a room."

"It won't be much different from this. Only smaller and not so noisy."

"Let's go to it, Mac."

I paid the check and we went out. There was a liquor store across the street and we went over and bought a bottle of whisky, crossed back again and went into the Crosley Arms. There were a couple of seedy-looking salesmen sitting in the lobby and the clerk was busy with a racing form. We walked to the elevator and I pushed the button for the fifth floor. Cynthia stood with her bag in her two hands in front of her, her eyes on the floor. Just before we stopped she looked at me suddenly, shyly and said, "The birds and the bees."

"These are the places some girls learn everything they know about them," I said.

She thought about it. "It might not be so bad if you could work into it gradually," she said. "But it's awful having to learn the whole lesson in twenty-four hours."

I wasn't sure what that meant, but I decided not to probe it.

The elevator stopped. We got out and I guided her down the dark hall to the last door on the right.

"Wait here a minute," I said.

I went in, around the end of the bed, lifted the spread and found the cut in the mattress. I reached in and felt the solid binding of the book. I went back to the door, switched on the light and nodded her in. I opened a window and pulled down the shade. She stood in the middle of the room looking around and refrained from sniffing.

"Honestly, Mac—it's the first time I've ever been in a place like this. I've read about them, seen them in the movies, but I've never been in one."

"Make yourself comfortable on the chaise longue," I said, "and I'll fix you a drink. Soda or ginger ale?"

"Ginger ale," she said.

I poured some whisky into a glass, ran some tap water in on top of it and handed it to her. She dropped her bag on the bed and sat down on the edge of it. The springs clanged. I stuck the pillows up against the headboard and she squirmed up that way and leaned against them, sipping her drink. I poured myself a shot, swallowed it and sat down in the chair.

"About the hole in the book," I said.

"The book is mine," she said. "It was given to me by my mother. It's been in my mother's family for generations. There's no need to go into the long story of how it came to our family. Of course, this one is only half the complete edition. Originally we had both volumes. But in 1871 my great grandmother's house was directly in the path of the Fire and the other volume was destroyed. This one was saved by a faithful family servant who knew how my great grandmother prized it."

"How much is it worth, in money?" I asked.

"This one volume—I don't know. A complete set in good condition was sold twenty years ago for over a hundred thousand dollars."

I shook my head. "Not enough," I said.

"Not enough for what?"

"For murder."

"I should think not. By the way, where is the book?"

"It's safe," I said. "Until everything is over, I think you'd be just as well off not knowing."

After a moment she nodded. "All right, Mac... When I married Warfield, mother gave me the book and asked me to keep it. Maybe she thought it would be a comfort to me. Sometimes, you know, it was. I kept it on a little nightstand beside my bed. My—Warfield—never paid any attention to it. It was mine. I don't remember that he ever mentioned it."

I fixed her another drink.

"When I decided to leave him a couple of weeks ago it was on the spur of the moment. I'd been spending the week end with friends in Wisconsin. They brought me home and on an impulse I asked them to wait, ran in and got an extra wrap and a couple of dresses and left without saying a word. I didn't think to take the book.

"Then the other—was it really only last night?—I remembered it and some other things and that was when I decided to drive out and get them. I checked the room quite carefully, and nothing else had been disturbed. But the book was gone. I was upset about it, but I didn't want to go to Warfield and after I'd found him there—in the library—I was too shocked to think to look for it. I didn't even think about it when you brought it to the apartment. I had it back and that was all that mattered. But when you left me this morning and said something about the pages being cut, I remembered."

"The reason it wasn't in your room," I said, "was that by then Alex had already delivered it to me."

"I see that. But that doesn't explain why the pages were cut."

"No, it doesn't. That is a piece of the story we don't know yet. And until we do know, I guess you're better off in what we might call protective custody."

She opened her eyes. Wide.

"Don't get excited," I said. "Donovan is no longer after you. You'll be safer with the cops than with me or by yourself."

"But what is there to be afraid of now, Mac?"

"There's stuff going on you don't know about. I'm going downstairs to call Donovan. Keep the door locked, to avoid any drunks that might wander in. I'll be right back."

I reached for the door and she caught at my hand. I sat down on the edge of the bed beside her.

"Tell me, Mac. Tell me what's going on? I've got a right to know."

"All right, here's some of it. Burnett wanted to make a deal for the book. I suggested twenty-five thousand bucks. He took too long to make up his mind and we had a little tussle. Later Marilyn Mayfair offered me thirty thousand. All day guys have been following me around—same organization that's been tailing you. After you called me tonight, I had to shoot a hole in one man's hand and push a couple of other guys out of the way, just to get out of my office.

"Behind all this is somebody named Garcia. A character built like a mountain in fancy clothes. They killed Alex. They kept their eye on you all the time the cops couldn't even find you and they have made life very inconvenient for me. Alone I can maybe outrun them. With you—there are too many of them."

Her eyes were going over my face. She reached up suddenly and touched my eyes. I winced. She raised onto her elbow and ran her hand lightly over my face, touching it here and there.

For a few minutes then, what I felt and what was in her eyes didn't have anything to do with the book or Donovan or Garcia or anything except the two of us. I guess she'd never been really kissed—anyway not by a private cop in a lousy cheap hotel room. She was stiff and awkward at first with her nose getting in the way and then I felt her relax and found her mouth and she was all yielding and sweet and warm.

"Let's stay, Mac. Let's not call the police or go anywhere. Let's stay here where nobody will bother us, just—being alone together."

"If you think I don't want to," I said, "you're crazy. But it wouldn't work, baby. Even if you're not wanted for murder, there are formalities. The police still have to talk to you. And a hotel room is a cinch to locate. It's not the same as moving around. When they want you, they'll come around. And we won't be private any more."

"Well then—until they come—" I twisted her nose.

"I never saw it fail," I said. "You treat a woman nice and right away she starts an argument."

She looked ashamed. "All right, Mac. You run the show."

I pulled out my gun and handed it to her.

"Like before," I said. "Use it if you have to. I'll only be gone a minute and I don't expect you'll have to. If you should—it would be well to determine first whether it's cops. You shoot a cop and they shoot you right back at the first opportunity."

I twisted the key, opened the door. "Lock this after I'm gone," I said. "And don't fall asleep."

She just looked at me. It made it hard to leave.

"There's only one reason I can think of to cut such a neat hole out of the middle of a book," I said. "And there aren't many types of things you can hide in that amount of space."

She didn't say anything and I went out, pulling the door shut after me. As I walked away down the hall I heard the click of the key and the bolt sliding home.

I had to wait a couple of minutes for the elevator. I shared it going down with a cockeyed lady in a red satin dress who hiccoughed regularly at intervals of three or four seconds. Halfway down she said without warning, "Hi, Mac."

It startled me.

"Do I know you?" I said.

"My God! Is that really your name? Imagine that!" She laughed like crazy.

I got out at the lobby and found a pay telephone in the corner. I dialed Donovan's private office number and one of his assistants came on.

"Hello, Samuel," I said. "Donovan in?"

"Who's asking?"

I told him.

"Oh—hi, Mac. No. He's out fishing."

"He know what he's trying to catch?"

"I think he does, Mac."

"Who?"

"Ah—you know better than to ask me."

"Sure. Look, Samuel. There are two things you can do for me."

"I can?"

"First, you can send a detail to the Crosley Arms Hotel to pick up Mrs. Warfield."

"But we don't want Mrs. Warfield any more."

"Mrs. Warfield wants you."

There was some silence.

"Oh. What's the matter, you slipping?"

"No. Just busy. Will you do it?"

"All right. She'll have to come in sooner or later. Might as well be now."

"I'll wait till they come. Here's the other thing—"

"I haven't got much time, Mac—"

"This won't take long. Look up in your 'Unsolved Larceny File' for the last couple of months—"

"We don't have any 'Unsolved' files."

"All right. Look where it tells you what got stolen and from whom and what the insurance companies paid off on, without reference to whether or not it was recovered by the cops. That sound better?"

"Much better. Local stuff?"

"Maybe. I'll hold the phone."

I waited two or three minutes. There was a rattle of papers at the other end and Samuel said, "This is a fat file, boy. Can you narrow it down?"

"I'll try. Jewelry—almost certainly. Value great."

"One piece or several?"

"Don't know."

"That helps a lot."

"Think of it this way: enough stuff to fit in a space about four inches square and one inch deep. If it's more than one piece, they're probably good sized. No little items that would slip under and get lost."

I heard him shuffling through the file. He started to say something, changed his mind and shuffled some more. Finally he said, "What about this? Three weeks ago a state museum in the Southwest reported the theft of an ancient Aztec gem during renovations to the building. Estimated value, one million, one hundred thousand dollars. Part of the museum insurance was underwritten by a New York firm, the rest of it by Lloyd's. No pay-off yet. They're still looking. We got the file because one of the suspects is a local boy named Callahan. We keep looking for Callahan, but he doesn't show up. Nobody's seen him for years. Used to be one of Scarpone's boys back in the twenties. Quite an operator. Played cards a lot —on boats. Different boats, same cards."

"What did he look like?"

"Like an Irishman."

"No kidding."

"Big fellow. Pale face. Curly black hair. Handsome devil. Great ladies' man. Listen, Mac. You got a line on this? The insurance examiner is pestering the devil out of the boys—"

"I don't have anything on it. Yet. Describe that gem—that Aztec thing."

"Let's see—emerald, carved in the form of a chalice. What's that?"

"A cup. Go on."

"Surrounded by six gold chains. Around the—outermost gold chain are six perfect pearls. Fancy piece."

"How big is it?"

"Whole thing measures three inches across, approximately three-quarters of an inch thick."

"A million bucks?"

"That's what it says. The thing was known as the 'Stone of Na—hua'—something like that. Got enough?"

"I guess so."

"Let us know if you find anything, huh?"

"Sure. You let me know if you find this Callahan."

"O.K. So-long, Mac, I'll send over for Mrs. Warfield."

"So-long, Samuel."

I hung up, went back and got in the elevator. It took it forever to get to the fifth floor. I'd been gone longer than I'd planned and I found I wanted to get back. When it finally stopped, the grating jammed and I had to jerk it off the track to get out. The guests would have to walk up and downstairs till they got it fixed.

I walked toward the jog in the wall where the hall to the back of the building narrowed down. I stopped. There was a draft blowing toward me, a draft of fresh air. When I'd left, the air had been stale and still. Also there was a minor jangle of sound. I stood behind the foot-wide jog of wall and looked around it into the narrow hall.

It took one look to convince me I was helpless. There were two of them, with her in the middle. One of them was just stepping through the window. Cynthia stood square in the middle of the window, half shielding the one climbing out. The other guy stood half in our room, half in the hall in a deep shadow. I could barely make out the line of his hat brim.

Which would have been enough if I'd known what Cynthia was going to do. I could maybe shoot him, if I were lucky enough to miss Cynthia. Then the guy beyond the window would come in behind Cynthia and I would be cooked. I could yell and either they would both come after me behind Cynthia, or the place would be jammed with a lot of curious guests.

Anyway I looked at it, the only smart thing I could do was to stand there with my hands in my pockets, watching them.

She wasn't making any fuss. But then I wouldn't expect her to. I wondered why she hadn't shot them and I had to admit that she probably had reasons. After what I'd told her, she would lean over backward to avoid shooting a cop. Although anybody ought to know the cops wouldn't be coming in off the fire escape. Only how would she know where they'd come from?

One of the guys said, "What about that shamus?"

"Screw him," said the other one. "I don't want to tangle with him in this hall anyway. He'll be along when he finds the dame gone."

He sounded like that wide-faced henchman of Burnett's.

Cynthia started to climb through the window. The guy in the doorway grabbed her arm, slid behind her, pulling her around, and went through the window first, leaving her framed there to be my only final target. He was smart. If he'd played it any other way he'd have got shot in the back. By me.

Cynthia swung her legs out over the windowsill. I saw her for a moment with the wide one beside her, then they all disappeared.

I ran down the hall on tiptoe. They were still too close for me to look out. I could hear their feet scraping on the steps. I grabbed a minute to duck into our room, feel around on the bed. Nothing there, except the faintly warm depression where she'd been lying. I slid my hand under the pillows, clamped on the butt end of my gun. I went around to the other side, reached into the mattress and pulled out the book. I went back to the hall window.

Little by little I stuck my neck out. The black iron grill of the fire stairs zigzagged downward to the alley behind the hotel. Everything was black —the wall of the building, the stairs, the alley below. They were wearing black suits. Once every few seconds I thought I could see a flicker of white that would be Cynthia's blouse.

I climbed through the window onto the platform and stared down. I could feel the old iron frame give and creak as they moved on it. Then a car swung around the corner and in the reflection of its headlights against the opposite building I saw their shapes two stories down. I started down the stairs, hugging the wall and crouching on the exposed sections, running down fast when they doubled back away from the street side of the hotel.

A big green Packard was parked across the street opposite the alley. I was on the second floor when its headlights flashed and the three of them below me ran from the base of the steps out across the street toward the car. Each guy held one of Cynthia's arms. They went fast and when she stumbled once, instead of slowing to let her get back on her feet, they dragged her the last few feet and pushed her into the back seat.

My feet hit the alley as the Packard began to move. Fifty feet behind it came a cab. That was too close—unless—And the light changed, the Packard turned left and out of sight on the yellow, and I pounded the pavement to where the taxi sat, waiting for the next change.

I only made it because some slow poke held up the cross stream. I yanked the door open, flopped onto the seat and told the driver, "Keep that Packard in sight all the way."

He caught on. We twisted left into Clark Street, a block and a half behind the Packard.

CHAPTER 11

The cabbie got a little over-enthusiastic and I had to slow him down.

"I don't want to get too far back," he said.

"You don't want to get too damned close either," I said.

"I don't?"

"You don't."

"Anything you say."

I had figured it for a short ride. Across the river, turn here and turn there, Mobile Club and there we'd be. But I was wrong. They worked over to the Boulevard and stayed right on it. And when they left it they were on the Drive, still headed north.

It wasn't a pleasant ride, because I didn't know what was going on in that back seat. I began to dream. If they got far enough out and the cab could get around in front I might be able to shoot a couple of tires off and slug it out right there.

That wasn't any good. They'd probably get me first.

I thought about getting up close, climbing on top of the Packard and picking them off one at a time through the windows. Then I had a picture of me trying to hold on to the top of the car while they went around a curve. I thought of some more but none of them was any good and I wound up just sitting on the edge of the seat, making sure we kept them in sight.

The traffic thinned gradually and we had to keep dropping back. A mile and a half south of Warfield's place at a big intersection, a Ford station wagon turned into the Drive ahead of us and followed the Packard.

"Now you got two," I said. "One's as good as the other."

"What if they separate?" he asked.

"Stick to the Packard."

But they didn't separate. The Ford was crowding the Packard as they passed Warfield's, and then suddenly they both disappeared.

"Pull up here," I said.

We slid to a stop in front of Warfield's gate.

"Where did they go?" the cabbie asked.

"In the lake," I said. "How much?"

He looked at the meter. "Seven-fifty."

I gave him ten and advised him to make a U-turn and get back to town. He made the turn and I don't know where he went after that.

It was a dark night, without a moon, but also without fog. I walked along the wall in front of Warfield's place, holding the book under one arm.

At the corner of the wall, where the old abandoned road led back toward the bluff, I stopped and took my time looking around. The trees and brush were heavy beyond the road and in there it was pitch black. There was a light streak where the road ran and a shadow along the base of the wall on the near side.

That was all geography. Human beings I didn't see. I stood still by the corner of the wall listening and I didn't hear anyone. After a while I looked around the corner pillar and I didn't see anyone. I stepped into the near shadow and held my free hand against the wall to guide myself over the uneven ground beside the road. The book was a nuisance. I tried to remember why I'd brought it. But it hadn't been a definite thought, just a kind of hunch that maybe, if we needed a ransom, we'd better have it handy. It was going to be a hell of a ransom though, with that hole where the ice was supposed to be.

Because that had to be it. Somehow Warfield had the stone, swiped Cynthia's book to hide it in. But where had it gone?

Anyway it was a nice friendly practical joke to play on your wife. Like dragging her around behind a boat, for shark bait. I was dreaming up some beautiful methods of killing sharks.

I stepped on a stick that broke with a loud crack. I stopped, hugged the wall and waited a minute. But nothing happened, so apparently they didn't have anybody posted down this way. That made it easier and I speeded up.

The Ford station wagon was parked so close I had to squeeze through sideways with my shoulder blades scraping the wall. Ahead of the Ford stood the Packard, not quite so close.

I wondered why the road had looked so unused that morning when I'd driven out with the poker. There must be another entrance farther on up the Drive. Or in back from the lake. With a fast boat you could get away from here unobserved and be in South Haven in two or three hours.

There was nobody in either of the two cars. I got to the wire stretching across the end of the road and stooped under it. From here on there wasn't any gray ribbon to guide me. It was through the woods, and I was no Indian.

But there was a path. If I couldn't see it I could feel it, a sort of tramped down, narrow walk with bushes and high grass on each side. I could put out my foot and, if it ran into a bush or a clump of grass, I could move it to one side or the other and find the path. By that method I felt my way along. It was slow, but it had to be right—unless they'd walked along the top of the wall.

The woods got thicker and the black blacker and I didn't seem to be getting anywhere. I pictured the path going in a wide circle and leading me back to the Drive. That scared me. I stopped and looked back. After a long time I made out a dull gleam that had to be the hood of the Packard. So I hadn't got twisted yet.

After that I concentrated on direction, noting the way my toe pointed with each step. I noted it so hard that I found myself suddenly tangled up in a row of high hedge before I understood what I'd struck. I backtracked. It was a head-high hedge, overgrown with a lot of other vegetation and probably impenetrable. It stretched away high and back to my left as far as I could see. To the right it appeared to run up against the Warfield wall. But it probably didn't. It made a more or less even line across the sky, which was all I could see beyond it.

I turned toward the Warfield wall and walked beside the hedge, looking for an opening. Twenty paces along there was a hole, not big enough to crawl through, but something to look through. I looked and beyond the hedge was a cleared space maybe fifty feet deep and beyond that windows with shades drawn and light leaking out around the edges. I went on.

The entrance was next to the wall around the Warfield place. There was an iron post at the end of the hedge and another post against the Warfield wall. There was no sign of the gate that had once hung between the posts.

I stood at the end of the hedge and studied the clearing. There was no cover of any kind between the hedge and the house. The house seemed to be the English cottage type, low and rambling with overhanging eaves and vines all over everything. I couldn't tell where the front door was. About halfway along the front wall of the house, five and a half feet up from the ground there was a glowing cigarette. I wondered whether there would be one on the back wall, too. Because that was where I was going.

With my eyes on the cigarette I stepped across the space between the hedge and the wall into the shadow. The cigarette glowed but didn't move. I squatted, laid the book down against the wall by the iron post and straightened up. It felt better moving with a gun in one hand instead of the book.

It was all grass along the wall and I didn't make any noise. There were twenty-five feet of space between the wall and the side of the house. The casement windows on the side were blank. Some of the panes were broken and ivy had climbed around the jagged edges. The low-hanging eaves cast a shadow along the wall of the house and, with the line of vision between the cigarette and me cut off by the corner of the building, I figured it was safe to cross over.

Now I could feel with my left hand and carry the gun in my right, which was where it should be. I had to stoop to keep from banging my head against the eaves.

The side wall of the house was maybe thirty feet deep. I went to the back corner. The grounds went on back forty or fifty feet to the edge of the lake bluff. I looked around the corner. There was a back wall running some thirty feet to a rear extension of the house that stuck out almost to the edge of the bluff. A little way this side of the extension was a lighted window. Between it and me were two more dark casement windows. So this side of the house would be the wall of an end room and the lights were coming from a room beyond near the middle of the house.

A door opened in the rear extension and somebody stepped out, closing the door behind him. A match flared, moved toward a cigarette and in the glow I saw the face of Lefty—the man who'd shot Alex in front of my office.

I backed up along the side wall as far as the casement window. There was a broken pane near the bottom and I reached for the hook. It could either make a lot of noise or break off in my hand. But there was going to be noise sooner or later and it might as well start now.

With one eye on the back corner, where Lefty's cigarette would show if he came, I heaved on the hook. It stuck and I gave it a slow, steady pull. It broke loose with no more than a light "Pfft" and I pulled outward until there was room to get a grip on the window frame. I lifted it, to ease the friction of the old rusted rods, and pulled it open. It squeaked some.

I swung a leg over the sill and was pulling the other one in after me when Lefty's cigarette came around the back corner. I flopped onto the floor under the window, reached up and pulled it to and waited.

He came on to the window, paused, glanced in over and beyond me, and went on. I lowered the gun. He might never know how close he'd come to having a hole in the head. Later I would tell him. Maybe.

When my eyes got used to it I saw that this room was empty of furniture. Straight across from the window there was a yellow line of light along the floor and three feet above it a little yellow keyhole. I crossed on my hands and knees and assumed the time-honored posture of my profession.

It was a big room, almost bare. The light came from two kerosene lanterns hung on wall brackets. There were some boxes here and there and one very old, dilapidated overstuffed rocker.

In the rocker sat the big guy with the brown face. I could see his profile and his hands on the arms of the chair. In front of him stood Cynthia.

She stood very straight, without seeming to be afraid of much of anything and there was a guy on each side of her, not touching her, just standing there. One of the guys was Al, whose finger I'd chewed on—it was still bandaged—and the other was the boy with the wide face that needed a shave.

On a box against the wall behind Cynthia sat Burnett. Across the room on another box was Miss Mayfair. Leaning against a door at the far end of the room was the little brown-skinned ragamuffin who had lifted Cynthia's bag out of my car early that morning.

The big boy in the chair was talking.

"Your husband, Mrs. Warfield, whose death I find myself regretting more and more, lent me a hundred thousand dollars on the security of that stone, a trifle of course, considering its real value. It was agreed that I would reclaim it within two weeks, paying him the hundred thousand plus interest."

"You were a fool to trust him," Cynthia said.

"I never trusted him, Mrs. Warfield. Let's say I required funds in a hurry, that it was impossible to sell the stone at the moment in the legitimate market and that through past associations I had cause, if not to trust him, at least to believe he had a certain respect for my resourcefulness. He knew I had means at my disposal for making life highly uncomfortable for him if he tried to cheat me.

"We know that your husband secreted the stone in the book, which is your property. We know that he sent the book to you, by way of the private detective known as 'Mac.' We watched very closely. Somewhere along the way we lost sight of the book. But we never lost sight of you, Mrs. Warfield, not for a minute, even while you paused at the Crosley Arms. Your tender scene with the detective was entertaining, but not sufficiently revealing. It was necessary to bring you here."

Cynthia's voice was bored.

"I'm sure it's a story that will fascinate your grandchildren. But what do you want of me?

"All I want of you is to know where the book is. About the book itself I care nothing and you may keep it.

He heaved himself out of the chair and stood looking down at her. He was so big that for a minute I couldn't see anything but him.

"But I want the stone. And I mean to have it."

She looked him straight in the face. "I don't know where the book is," she said. "And I don't know where the stone is."

"Forgive me, please," he said, "but it is incredible to me that you would leave anything so valuable as an original Gutenberg Bible to the tender mercies of a cheap keyhole peeper."

"He's not a cheap keyhole peeper!" she said. "And he is certainly more clever than you, who have tried—how many times?—to bribe, beat or trap him."

She was brave and scornful and tough and all the things she'd been trained to be. But she was clearly not wise. That stuff only destroys what little patience exists in guys like him, and his had run out already.

He looked at her with his lips working for a minute and then he swung the back of his hand against her face, twisting to get his weight into it.

"You're a fool, Mrs. Warfield," he said.

She fell toward the wide guy who pushed her back up and held her arm, while Al held the other. She drooped between them, sagging in the knees, and then little by little she straightened up and lifted her head to look back at him.

I twisted the doorknob silently, held it tightly, checked to make sure the safety catch was off the gun, and then pushed on in.

"Everybody just stand still," I said, "with the hands up.

The little brown man across the room didn't get them up fast enough. I sent one into the doorjamb, burning his cheek. He got them up.

I pushed the door shut behind me and leaned against it. Burnett was the one I had to be afraid of and I spent most of the time watching him.

"Can you walk, baby?" I asked.

"Yes," Cynthia said.

"Then walk straight back to the wall beyond Mr. Burnett there."

She backed up to the wall. She was out of range of any move that might come. I talked to the big one.

"Señor—Callahan?" I asked.

He didn't answer.

"You got two boys outside. Call 'em. Tell them to come in the front way and through the door where that little man is standing across the room. Right now. As loud as you can yell."

It was pretty loud. He yelled the whole message. And it was a good thing because my hand was trembling on the gun and my fingers weren't under the best control. He must have noticed it.

After a minute the little brown man moved away from the door, it opened and one guy came in. He was a little brown man, too. I couldn't tell whether he'd lost his tongue or not but otherwise they looked like brothers.

"Where's Lefty?" I asked.

Nobody seemed to know.

"Call him again," I said.

He did.

I was watching Callahan, figuring him to be the control factor. I counted to three, waiting to hear from Lefty.

But what I heard came from Cynthia.

"Mac!" she screamed.

She yelled it loud enough but she neglected to explain where to look. There was the slap of a window shade and when I looked that way Lefty's gun was sticking through a broken pane in the front window and Lefty's voice was saying, "Drop the heater, shamus. I can blow a hole right through the girl with this."

I'd seen him in action and I knew he could. I dropped the gun, cursing myself for not drilling him when he passed that side window.

Burnett had a rod out, trained on me.

"Want me to come in?" Lefty asked.

"Stay out there," Callahan said. He stabbed a finger at one of the little brown guys. "You go out, too."

The little man disappeared. Burnett walked up to me, kicked my gun across the floor and pulled me away from the wall.

"Come over and join the party," he said.

The little scar beside his nose was red now, not white. His eyes were full of blood and it was all hot. He pushed me over against the wall beside Cynthia. We didn't look at each other.

"Hello, baby," I said.

"Hello, Mac."

That was all we had time for. The boy with the wide face took Burnett's gun and held it on Cynthia. Burnett looked into my face and said, "Where is it?"

I looked past him. He hit me three times. My head banged the wall each time. Cynthia drew in her breath.

"Mac," she said. "Tell them. For God's sake. It's not worth all this."

"I can tell you where the book is," I said. "That's all."

He hit me again. He was doing it now because he enjoyed it. There wasn't any other reason.

"Don't talk so much," he said. "Just tell me where it is."

"Stop it!" Cynthia said.

Burnett moved over and slapped her. He was having himself quite a time.

"It's out there by the old gate beside Warfield's wall," I said, "at the base of the iron post."

Callahan gave a signal. The door opened and the little brown guy slipped out. There was a complete silence. Burnett stood in front of me, stroking his knuckles. The wide-faced guy held the gun steady on Cynthia and Al stood beside Burnett. Callahan sat in his chair.

When the door opened, he got up. He waited while the little one came across the room and stuck the package in his hand. He turned it over two or three times, then tore the wrapping off, in handfuls, feverishly, dropping the paper on the floor.

All this time there had been neither sound nor motion out of Mayfair. Now she got up from the box and came across the room to stand beside Callahan. Burnett didn't move.

Callahan leafed through the book, his big hands clumsy. Suddenly the pages stopped turning. He was holding the book open, staring at it. He stared for quite a while, then his hands relaxed and the book fell to the floor.

"It's gone," he said, and his voice was far away.

This was the moment I'd been waiting for, knowing it had to come. This was where I had to talk fast, thinking ahead of them. They would have no idea about anything except that Cynthia and I had taken the stone out and put it somewhere else. I had figured out most of it, but there were some points that were pretty fuzzy and I would have to make them sound right.

But I didn't get started soon enough. Burnett was all primed.

"I thought it came too easy," he said.

Al and the wide one grabbed me then, one on each side and dragged me out from the wall, twisting me around to face Cynthia. Burnett had his back to her. Nobody was watching her for a moment. And instead of standing there quietly like a good, smart girl, she lifted her foot, slipped off her shoe and banged Burnett over the back of the head with the heel of it.

It wasn't hard enough. It only raised his temperature. He turned around and while Al and the other one held me very tight, he threw his fist into Cynthia the way a man pitches a baseball underhand.

I closed my eyes. I heard her fall and there was a great absence of sound after she'd fallen. When I opened my eyes Burnett had turned back to me. It had to be now.

"Wait a minute," I said. "You've all been so busy double-crossing each other you haven't figured anything out."

It didn't stop Burnett. He kept coming at me. But Callahan stepped in between, pushing Burnett out of the way.

"Go ahead," Callahan said. "Talk some more."

"Burnett offered me twenty-five thousand bucks for the book."

Burnett screamed, "He's a goddamned liar!" and tried to come around Callahan, who held him off the way you'd fend off a puppy.

"Mayfair offered me thirty thousand."

Callahan looked at her.

"He's crazy," Mayfair said. "He's just trying to get us fighting among ourselves."

I kept my eyes on Callahan.

"There wasn't any stone in the book when Warfield sent it to me. I never saw the stone. I never even heard of it till I came in here tonight. And neither did Mrs. Warfield.

"If Warfield put the stone in the book, then he took it out again before he sent it to me. I don't know what kind of a game you're playing, but one of you here knows where the stone is and isn't telling. You'll have to work that out. But you can beat me to death and not get anywhere, because I don't know where the stone is. You say you don't either. But one of you is lying. Figure out which one and you'll know something."

Burnett and Mayfair were watching Callahan. Callahan was watching me. So when the door opened, nobody knew just where to look. And when we all got straightened out, looking at the same place, there was Donovan in the doorway, with Lefty behind him.

"I found this cop sneaking around in the brush," Lefty said.

"Alone?" Callahan said.

"There were a couple of others with him. They're layin' out there."

"Where's Pedro?"

"Dead," Lefty said. "This cop broke his back. With his hands."

Donovan stood there. There was a deep cut on his cheekbone and a line of blood running down under his jaw. His clothes were torn and rumpled. Lefty looked mussed up, too.

Donovan said, "I come here for one thing only. The one that knocked off Warfield. Not because I give a damn about Warfield. But just because I'm stubborn."

Callahan turned away. "You're in the wrong place, copper," he said.

"I don't think so," Donovan said. "Shall I start naming names?"

"Sure," Callahan said. "Give us a name."

Mayfair's voice shrilled across the room. "Miguel!" she said. "Did you hear what Lefty said? He broke Pedro's back, your own brother!"

It all happened very fast. Little Miguel moved as swiftly as a spider. Only spiders don't throw knives and this one was long and thin and only the black handle of it showed, sticking out of Donovan's back as he spilled forward onto the floor.

Miguel slipped through the door and disappeared.

Lefty's mouth was open. He stared down at Donovan, then he looked up and his eyes wandered around the room.

"Where's Miss Mayfair?" he asked, plaintively, as if things were moving too fast for him.

Callahan and Burnett both wheeled around, stared at each other.

"There's only one place it could be," Callahan said.

"Warfield's place," said Burnett.

They made for the door.

"Hey!" Al shouted.

Burnett turned.

"Stay here and watch the shamus," he called.

"The hell with that," Al said. "You think I don't know you? You won't come back."

The boy with the wide face was already crowding Burnett out the door. There was a movement behind me and something crashed against the side of my head.

I never heard Al run across the room to catch up with the others.

CHAPTER 12

I woke up in the dark. The floor was cold under me and everything was dark. But there was warmth close to me. It floated near my face in little slow puffs of warm air. Pretty soon I could hear it, too. It was breathing—conscious, irregular breathing.

I was having the devil of a time remembering. My head kept expanding and contracting. It would swell up to the splitting point, hover around there for a while, then it would contract, squeeze itself down to the size of a match head and all the screwy images in it would contract proportionately and get far away and disappear. Then it would start to swell up again. Every time the swelling started I would be sick to my stomach, not enough to really heave anything out of it, but just on the verge.

At first I couldn't remember anything, except my head banging around. Then, working back from there, I began to piece things together. I straightened out the face of the man who'd been beating me and remembered Burnett.

I was lying on the floor of his office. Now I remembered. There was a jumble of other faces floating around and I worked hard on them. I got them pretty well sorted out and then they started to slip away again.

A hand touched my face.

That would be Marilyn Mayfair.

I felt myself jump, trying to get out from under the hand. And I must have made a noise because a voice came.

"Mac," it said, "Mac—are you all right?"

I lay very still, trying to place the voice. It was familiar, but it wasn't anybody I knew. One of those puffs of warm air had come with it. The warmth felt good and I reached out, trying to find it. I thought if I could get it in my hands and the voice too, I could identify it. I knew I would feel better if I could identify it, but I didn't know why. I felt for it, found it, stopped suddenly.

"Excuse me," I said.

I couldn't hear it. I thought it and I thought I said it. But I couldn't tell whether I had really said it aloud.

There were two hands this time, one on each side of my face and the warm air and the voice again, saying, "Mac—it's all right. It's Cynthia."

And I got it. And this time I heard myself say it.

"Mrs. Warfield," I said.

"That's right. Mrs. Warfield."

A lot of stuff came back then and I sorted it out fast and remembered things—a hotel room, the Tivoli Theater, taxicabs—all pretty jumbled up, but getting clearer. There was something way in the back that I kept trying to remember and couldn't. Something important. I couldn't remember it at all, or even what it had to do with. But the other stuff kept clearing up.

"Lie still, Mac. Take it easy," she said.

I couldn't see her—or anything. I opened my eyes, or thought I did, but I couldn't see anything.

"Dark," I said.

"I turned the lanterns out," she said. "I thought it would be better."

"Yeah," I said. "More private."

I lay still and thought. There were big bunches of things in the clear now. But every once in a while there would be a blank that was just a mass of clouds and each time one of those came along it drowned out everything I'd cleared up. It was like a hurdle race. Run like hell—all of a sudden there's a hurdle. How did those runners take them? One at a time. All right. Set 'em up, one at a time, sail right over. And to make sure I kept it clear I did it out loud.

"Garcia," I said, "was Callahan. Stole the rock in Arizona, New Mexico, somewhere. I think he pulled a con game down there to get close to it. Dyed his skin—posed as an Aztec or something. Kept the disguise up here because he was pretty hot.

"Knew Warfield in the old days, went to him and got money. Probably sold the stone outright. Figured to steal it back. Contacted Burnett and Mayfair to help.

"Mayfair saw Warfield hide the stone in the book. Warfield must have known that—or Alex knew and informed on Mayfair.

"Warfield took stone out of the book, but Mayfair didn't see that. Then he sent the book to you—hid the stone somewhere else. Hired me to deliver the book to you to make damn sure they knew he'd sent it. Mayfair knew he'd called me in."

It was hard work. I stopped, licked my lips to loosen them. "I don't suppose we've got anything to drink."

"No, Mac. I'm sorry. I know where it is next door, but not here."

"Losche was in on it, too. They held that debt over his head, led him around by the nose. I think it happened like this:

"Losche hung around outside while the murderer went in and got Warfield away from the library. Then he sneaked in, picked up the book and lammed out again, hid somewhere. Sprinkling system been on—how he got mud on his shoes."

I looked up. I could almost see her now.

"You think I'm crazy? How could he pick up the book when the book was already gone with Alex?

"The cigar box, baby. Warfield put the book in the cigar box. False bottom. I knew it should have moved more when I threw that knife in it. It was too heavy. There had to be something besides cigars. Then when we drove out there and found Warfield dead the box was gone.

"All right. Losche ran out with the box. Murderer couldn't fool Warfield long enough. Warfield went back, saw the box was gone, and got upset. Murderer struck him. He didn't die fast enough—had to be finished off with the poker.

"Chance to make it look like you then. Wronged wife—and all that. Murderer sent Losche to your place to plant the poker.

"It was Mayfair sicced Burnett onto me. I think Warfield told her he was hiring me to deliver the book. Double check to make sure they'd watch you and me instead of him.

"Burnett's a sharp boy. He knew Alex. When he saw him coming down the street to my place with the package, he put two and two together. He was right, but the timing was wrong. Lefty's trigger-happy. Shooting raises a fuss. This one raised a fuss so fast they didn't have time to get what they were after.

"After you paid Losche's debts, he was a menace instead of a slave. He had to be put to sleep, too. I guess he was just as well off."

Cynthia's hands rubbed my face. "That's enough, Mac. Rest now."

"I figured that all out. Pretty smart, huh?"

"Pretty smart."

I relaxed. I was sleepy. When she rubbed my face I got sleepier. But I couldn't stop talking.

"I remember sneaking up to a house where Callahan and Burnett and Mayfair were. But I can't remember what happened. Were you there?"

"Yes, Mac. I was there."

"Wait a minute—yeah. Burnett—" I tried to sit up. The room turned over.

"Lie still, Mac."

"Burnett slugged you. In the—stomach. Hey—what about that?"

"I'm all right, Mac. I hurt, but I'm all right. I woke up and saw you and I got up and turned off the lanterns. I walked around. If I can walk around I'm all right."

"I remember—everybody running out, and that Al slugged me."

That important thing in the back of my mind was still struggling to come through. But I was so sleepy I couldn't help it any. I just had to lie there and let it twist around, like a doctor's probe in a deep wound.

I'd have given in to the sleep if the probe hadn't suddenly dug too deep. The probe was her voice, saying, "Mac—who's the man lying over by the door, with the knife in his back?"

This time I sat up all the way and stayed up. I fought off the sickness and I pushed her hands off my chest.

"Yeah," I said. "That's it. That's what I was trying to remember."

Nothing was fuzzy any more.

"How long have we been here?" I asked. "How long was I out?"

"I don't know. When I came to I remember there were feet running outside. I don't know how long I've sat here with you."

"Does it seem long?"

"It seems awfully long."

"An hour? Two hours?"

"It seems like an hour anyway."

"Then it's maybe fifteen, twenty minutes. If we're lucky."

I got on my knees and crawled around on the floor, patting it, looking for my gun, the one Burnett had kicked away.

"If we're lucky," I said. "God, let me be lucky once tonight."

Cynthia was beside me, tugging at me.

"Mac, what is it? Please—what are you looking for? What's it about? Who is that man, Mac?"

"That's Donovan, baby."

"No, Mac."

"Yeah. My gun was right around here somewhere—Burnett kicked—ah!"

I picked it up, found a match in my pocket and handed it to Cynthia.

"Strike a light, baby."

She struck the match. I remembered firing once and I broke it, loaded it and slipped it into my pocket. I crawled over to the wall, braced myself against it and pushed up to my feet. I leaned there, getting accustomed to it. Cynthia stood up, too. She put her hands on my shoulders. Her voice was level, even and low. "What are you going to do, Mac?"

"I'm going to get the murderer of Donovan—and Warfield. What the hell did you think?"

"You're out of your mind, Mac. There are too many of them. We'll go call the police. It's their job—"

"No time for that, baby. If we're lucky—if it hasn't been too long—they're still over at Warfield's."

"But Mac—"

"I'm not taking the law into my own hands. I'm not going to shoot them in the back. I'm going to arrest them. The nice thing about that is—I don't think they'll come along without a fight. And in self defense, I'm going to have to do some damage."

Her hands dropped. "But you're—all alone, Mac."

"Sure. A guy like me, I'm always alone."

I took a couple of steps and I didn't fall down. So I was all right.

"Come on," I said. "We'll find a place to hide you."

"No."

"Don't argue. I'll love you, baby, but I won't argue. Is there any way into the place except that front gate?"

"Not from this side."

"Then it's over the wall. Can you do it?"

"If you can."

We crossed the room in the dark. Beside Donovan I knelt down. I couldn't just walk out on him, even now. I laid my hand on his shoulder.

He moved.

I stuck my hand in under his coat. There was a heart beating there somewhere. It was far away, but it was still going. I struck a match.

"Hello, shamus," Donovan whispered.

"Hello, copper."

Cynthia was on her knees beside me. Donovan looked at her, slanting his eyes up past me. "Mrs. Warfield?" he said.

"Yes—Donovan," she said.

"Pleased to meet you. Mac—did you get the one we want?"

"We want all of them," I said, "and I didn't get any of them."

He started to roll over. I grabbed him and eased him back down. His eyes closed and he rubbed the side of his face a little against the board floor.

"Get me a wad of cloth," I said to Cynthia.

Feeling carefully in the dark, I cut a hole in his coat and shirt around the knife handle. I heard cloth ripping and Cynthia shoved something into my hand.

"Light a match and hold it," I told her, "but don't look."

She lit the match. When the knife came out there was a long sigh from Donovan. I laid the pad of rayon cloth over the wound. After a couple of minutes Donovan said, "Get goin', shamus. You can't catch crooks hanging around here."

"All right," I said.

"Mac," Cynthia said. "Isn't there anything else we can do?"

"Not unless you happen to have some sulfa powder handy."

113

Donovan was wearing a shoulder holster. I managed to ease his gun out of it without moving him too much. I handed Cynthia the gun, guided her other hand to the pad of cloth in the middle of Donovan's back.

"I'll be back," I said. "Just keep the pad on there and if any of those people come back—this time use the gun."

"All right, Mac."

I couldn't see her in the dark, but her voice reminded me how she looked and it helped.

I went outside, stepped onto the grass and took some deep breaths. I wondered whether they'd killed those two cops who'd been with Donovan. They must have.

I started across the clearing toward the hedge, and stumbled over one of them. I leaned over, lit a match to see by. His name had been Williams. A good cop. Had a wife and two kids.

I threw away the match.

"O.K., pal," I told him. "For you, too."

I went to the end of the hedge where the old gate had been, tested the two-inch pipe beside the wall and found it solid.

Using my hands on the pipe and my toes on the wall, I made it to the top. I crawled across, twisted to get hold of the edge of the wall and dropped. I fell in the grass, rolled over and got up. Then I walked away from the wall toward the dark shape of the Warfield mansion.

CHAPTER 13

I couldn't tell whether I was in time until I got right up to it. I was on a line with the back wall of the house, nearly on the edge of the bluff, and from across the lawn, two hundred yards away, every window had been black. But when I got to within fifty feet of the back corner, there was a dull glow shining out of the back, from a window overlooking the lake. That would be Warfield's library.

I stayed close to the side wall and walked along toward the front. I'd gone twenty paces when somebody turned the corner up front and walked toward me. I stopped, waited for him.

He walked right into me. I kicked his feet out behind him, fell on him, got one arm around his throat, the other around his thighs.

"Just one little squeak," I said, "and it happens to you just like to brother Pedro."

He didn't move. I held onto the throat, released his legs and pulled him up. I stuck the rod in his back and pushed.

"It's too bad you can't talk," I told him, "but maybe you can do it some other way. Move along."

He walked. After a while he started to veer away from the wall. I rammed him up against it, tickled his throat with the gun.

"Stay close," I said, "or I'll stick this down your throat and blow a hole through your kidneys."

I meant every word of it.

He stayed close to the wall then. He walked right along for a while, and then he slowed down. He went slower and slower and just before we reached the front corner he stopped dead.

That was all I wanted to know. I laid the gun barrel against the back of his head and as he fell I pushed him out beyond the corner.

A voice said, "What the hell?"

Lefty was always saying that. He looked around the corner and I had my fingers in his eyes before he could focus on anything. He bent over, grabbing them, and I straightened him up, stole his gun and twisted him around to face the other way.

"No noise," I said. "We'll just walk along the wall here to the front door. Where's everybody?"

He didn't answer. He was too busy rubbing his eyes. I kicked him in the fanny.

"Where's everybody?"

"Inside," he said.

"Then we'll go inside, too."

"You can't make it. There's a guy on each side of the door inside. They'll cut you to pieces."

"Not me. Because you'll be going in first."

He walked along. Every once in a while I had to boot him along with my foot. It was fun. Made him madder than hell. But he didn't talk back.

A few feet short of the front portico I grabbed his neck and talked into his ear. "When we get close, you tell them you're coming in. Then go in brother. I'll be right behind you and I'm nervous as a witch tonight."

I let go of him and he went on to the edge of the portico.

"Al!... Lou!" he called. "It's Lefty. I'm comin' in."

"O.K.," Al said from inside.

We went up the steps. Lefty took hold of the door-knob, pushed and went in. The only light came from the half-open door of the library across the reception hall. It was enough light to see Al and Lou by—and for them to see me. They both jumped and I waved my heater at them and hissed. Lefty was between Al and me on the right. Lou was on the left. I had Lefty's gun in my left hand and I motioned to Lou to step around.

"Face that door," I whispered, "and drop the guns."

They did it. The guns made a lot of noise hitting the floor. There had been voices and rattlings of paper and one thing and another in the library. When the guns dropped that all stopped. There was a moment of silence.

Then Callahan called, "What's going on out there?"

Nobody answered. The door opened wider, throwing more light into the reception hall, and big-boy Callahan stood there. He looked at his three lads lined up in a row and he was puzzled. He looked at their guns on the floor and then, over somebody's shoulder, he looked at me.

"Oh—it's the shamus," he said. "What do you want?"

"You," I said, "and Burnett and Mayfair and these three little boys in front of me, for murder. You want to come along quiet?"

That was just a joke to him, as I'd figured it would be. He reached in behind his coat lapel.

"No!" Lefty screamed. "Don't go for it—!"

They held on there for about one second. That was all they could stand. Then they broke in all directions and I was pumping it into Callahan as fast as I could pump. He sagged outward, came halfway across the reception hall and tumbled on his face.

116

Al and Lefty were scooting up the stairs, Lefty way ahead. I caught him just before he disappeared. He hung there on the top step, weaving back and forth, then he rolled down, his arms flopping. Al stopped, lifted his hands and backed down the steps.

The other one, Lou, was trying to hide behind the edge of the big mirror. He was too big. His stomach stuck out. Al was at the bottom of the steps. So far Burnett and Mayfair hadn't shown up. It was all silence in the library.

"You two," I said to Al and Lou, "go get Burnett."

They stood very still.

"Go ahead," I said. "Bring him out."

Burnett spoke up for the first time, from inside the library. "Sure," he said. "Come on in boys."

They didn't move.

"I'm ashamed," I said. "Two big lads like you—afraid of your own boss and a girl."

Nothing happened. I wanted to shoot them where they stood, but I couldn't. I'd never done that. I called to Burnett.

"Mrs. Warfield is over in the servants' quarters," I said, "calling the cops. They'll be along any minute. You can come out now, peaceably, or we can all just stand around and wait."

"I'll wait," Burnett said.

I looked at Lou. I raised my voice. "You paid off the landlady at Losche's place and the guy in the gas station down the road."

He just shrugged. I put a slug in the mirror about shoulder high. A chip of glass flew off and cut across his cheek.

"Yeah," he said. "Yeah, I did."

"Who gave you the dough for it?"

He looked at the library door. I asked him again. He ran his tongue over his lips.

"Next piece of glass I knock out of there will go in your eye," I said. "Who gave you the dough?"

"All right," he said. "Don't shoot again. It was—" Lou had picked the wrong spot to hide. He was in line with the opening in the library door-jamb. I wasn't. They'd have to show to get at me.

Lou slid down into a big heap in the corner made by the wall and the mirror. Even after he was dead, he still needed a shave. I looked at Al.

"You're next," I said. "What do you want to say?"

"Honest," Al said, "I don't know nothing. No kidding. Give me a break. I didn't have nothing to do with any of it—except only what you saw."

He was shaking. He still had his hands up and his fingers were shaking like the morning after. That could have been because all the blood had run out of them. He started to lower them and I barked at him. He put them back up again.

Mayfair spoke up from inside the library.

"O.K., Mac," she called. "I quit. I'm coming out."

"Come right," I said, "or we'll have trouble."

The library door opened wider. Mayfair appeared, holding her hands up by her shoulders. She stood there a minute and looked at me, then walked out slowly into the reception hall.

She certainly was a beautiful hunk of woman. She looked bigger than I had realized before. Which was a good thing for Burnett, who was right behind her, close behind her. Too close for me to pick him off without hitting her.

I took a chance on the dim light, ducked and scooted across behind Al to the stairway. Burnett's gun barked from behind Mayfair and there was a sting in my thigh that broadened into a burn and stuck with me. The banister was set on those upright sticks four or five inches apart. Between a couple of them I saw Al streak for his gun, still on the floor, and I made sure of him first. He keeled over with a big "pouf" as the last of his breath went out of him.

Burnett was shooting like a crazy man. I lay on a step and let him use up his gun. He clicked it seven or eight times after he'd emptied it. Then he hit Mayfair in the head with it, to get her out of the way I guess, threw it at me and stepped over Mayfair across the reception hall.

I shot him in the leg and he went down on one knee. I dropped my gun in my pocket and went over the banister after him before he could get up. Then I helped him a little. When he was up he backed away from me, limping. He stumbled over Lou and I had to help him up again. This time he swung on me.

I pushed him into the mirror and the glass cracked around his shoulders.

He was sharp all right. I found he'd faked the limp and all of a sudden he was all over me and I was flat on my back. The place was so cluttered up with bodies I kept bumping into them when I tried to get up. I saw his foot coming down into my face and I grabbed and twisted. It must have been on the leg I'd hit because he hollered and flopped down.

I yanked him up and pushed him back against the side of the mirror frame. He struggled some and I took two or three nasty ones in the face, but then I got settled down and worked on his diaphragm and after a while he wasn't making any more passes. Just to keep it neat, I clipped his head once, good and hard. He didn't move a muscle. He didn't drop either, so I did it again. He was still standing there. I stood back and looked at him. His eyes were shut, his head was drooping, his hands hung down. But he was still up. I went around to the side. There was a big hook in the side of the mirror frame and somehow his coat had got snagged over it when I pushed him against it. He was just hanging there.

I left him there and looked around for Mayfair. She was standing in the doorway of the library, leaning against the jamb. There was a long bruise on the side of her head. I walked toward her, stopping under the staircase landing that ran across the hall ten or twelve feet up. She gave me one of those lazy smiles.

"Nice work, Mac," she said. "They had it coming. All of them."

"Yeah," I said. "Yeah, that's right. But they got off easy, at that. It won't be so easy—the way you'll have to take it."

Her smile didn't change. Only her position. She quit leaning and stood up.

"Why, you've got it all wrong, Mac," she said. "I don't understand you at all."

"I'll clear it up. It wouldn't matter about Warfield—even Losche maybe. I'd forget about them. But you murdered Donovan, too. That was a mistake. They'll see you dead for that."

"You're crazy. I was across the room from Donovan. You saw that Miguel kill him—with your own eyes."

"Sure. But that was just reflex-emotion. Miguel killed the man who killed his brother. But he wouldn't have, if you hadn't screamed at him. I don't think he even caught on about Pedro till you repeated it to him."

"And why would I do that?"

"Because Donovan was about to name you as Warfield's murderer."

"I was at the club. I appeared in both floor shows. Anybody will say so."

"You were in a show at 9:50. At ten o'clock you went to your dressing room, hung that 'Do Not Disturb' sign on the door, stepped into the alley, went around front and got in a cab. You picked Losche up somewhere and came out here. Took maybe forty minutes. You went in and got him on fire—a cinch for you—and he followed you upstairs. But he got to thinking and he cooled off all of a sudden and went back to the library. You followed him and when he saw the cigar box was gone, he went after you and you grabbed the knife and let him have it. Then you packed Losche off with the poker and beat it back to the club—in your own car, which had made a rapid recovery—in time to make the second show."

"That's a great story. Think you can make it stick? And what was that about Losche?"

"I don't know how you did that. I know when. It had to be about five minutes before Cynthia Warfield got there. She gave you a lot of breaks. You must have hid in Losche's closet when she came in. After she left you beat it down to where Lou was waiting and gave him one of those nice big bills to present to the landlady, to impress Mrs. Warfield on her mind."

"It's fantastic," she said.

"It was fantastic. Which is why it went wrong. You should have left it to Burnett."

Her eyes shifted from my face, looked over my shoulder, widened. There was an explosion behind me, and then a sprawly thing, all arms and legs, floated down beside me and spread out on the floor. I looked down.

It was brown little Miguel with a long knife in his hand. I wondered if he hatched them.

I looked around. Cynthia was standing in the front doorway, staring at the gun in her hand. The library door slammed and when I looked, Mayfair was gone.

"Mac—she's—"

"Let her go. She can't go far enough to get away. What about Donovan?"

"He's all right. At least, more worried about you than himself. He told me you'd need help... I thought he was kidding."

I went to her. She held the gun limply in her hand, staring across the hall at Miguel.

"He was crawling over the railing—with that knife—" She leaned against my chest and I held her. Outside I heard sirens.

"How will they get in?" I asked.

"The button is in the vestibule beside the front door."

I left her, went into the vestibule and pushed the button. Then I went back. We stood there waiting. After a few minutes there was a roar of cars out front, a screech of brakes and feet on the steps. The door opened and a sergeant from homicide came in along with a couple of sheriff's deputies. The sergeant looked around.

"My god!" he said, "what a mess."

He saw us.

"Who are you? Oh—hello, Mac."

"Boys got a little upset," I told him.

"Take it a step at a time," he said, "and tell me all of it."

"Tomorrow," I said. "You better go next door first. Donovan's over there with a hole in him."

His face became expressionless. "Dead?"

"No. But I wouldn't waste any time."

He went out front and I heard him talking to somebody out there. A car started, went away fast on the drive. The sergeant came back in. He prowled around, looking at the dead faces. Finally he went over to where Burnett hung on the hook in the mirror. His hands went under Burnett's bunched-up coat. He turned around. "This one's still alive," he said.

"Yeah?" I said. "Well—he's a tough boy. I don't think he'll say anything to help you."

"Yes, he will," the sergeant said. "He'll say something. It may take a while. But he'll say something."

"Find anything?" I asked him.

"No... Wait—here's something."

He brought it over, holding it in the palm of his hand. It didn't show off much in that light, looked like a round piece of tin with some crystal here and there.

"What is it?" asked the sergeant.

"Some little bauble," I said. "They say it's worth a million bucks."

"No kidding. That little thing?"

"Give it to Samuel in Donovan's office," I said. "He knows about it. That's what all this fuss was about... That's why Burnett and the broad came out instead of waiting for you lads. They'd found it and they made a play to get away with it."

"What broad?"

"I forgot. Mayfair. She went back in there. Be careful when you go after her. She's kind of mean."

"Is there any other way out of that room?"

Cynthia spoke up. "No," she said. "In the whole house, each room had only one door. The windows in the library overhang the bluff. There's a sheer drop to the lake."

"Then if you go after her," I told the sergeant, "and she's not in there, you'll have to look in the lake."

The two deputies were standing in the shadows near the front door. The sergeant nodded at them and they followed him across the reception hall toward the library door, picking their way carefully.

I looked at Cynthia.

"Something about a drink?" I said.

"Yes, Mac. Upstairs."

Her sitting room upstairs was as large as her whole apartment on Sheridan Road. We sat side by side on a sofa, drinking straight Scotch.

"For a long time," I said, "I couldn't figure out why Warfield gave me all that phony build-up when I went to see him. Now I think I know. He was a guy never trusted anybody in his whole life. A time came when he had to find somebody he could leave alone to do a job and know it would

121

get done. He offered me a fantastic price to tail you around. When I turned that down, he figured I was straight.

"He had a crook's mind all his life."

I took another drink.

"Mayfair had a lot of the wrong kind of guts," I said. "It took quite a lot to tussle with Warfield, and then to wipe her fingerprints off the handle of the knife while it was still in him."

Cynthia put her hand on my arm. "Don't talk about it any more, Mac. It's all over."

"Yeah—it's all over."

She was very close and that warmth in her went all over me. I stood up and she stood with me.

"All of it," I said.

I walked across to the door and she came after me.

"Mac—the part of it that's just between us, is that over too?"

"That, too."

"Does it have to be?"

"It has to be, baby. A girl like you and a guy like me—" The look of her stopped me, the way her head went up, tough and straight, all that stuff they'd drilled into her.

I opened the door. If I'd stayed any longer I couldn't have left her.

"I'll ask one of the boys to drive you back to your apartment," I said. "So-long now."

She didn't make any fuss. "So long, Mac," she said.

I went out, and the warm thing in her voice went with me all the way.

Made in the USA
Las Vegas, NV
15 December 2020